## "Get them."

A gunshot rang out. Alexis ducked and put both hands over her head. A scream tore from her throat. The dog answered with a bark. The bullet snapped a branch. It spun and smacked her shoulder. The realization that she'd helped the men pinpoint their location hurt more than her throbbing shoulder.

Nick grabbed her wrist and pulled her around a second trunk. He kept his fingers there, pulling, silently urging her to run faster, but her sandals didn't have much grip. Alexis fought the surge of nausea as several men's voices filtered through the trees. "Use the jammer," one shouted.

"Shoot only on sight. We don't need the whole valley showing up!" It sounded like the voice of the man who had confronted them at the house, but she couldn't be sure.

She slipped her hand in her pocket and, using tiny movements, tried to fish her phone out. The slash through the image of the cell tower on the screen confirmed her fear. No help would be coming. They were alone.

**Heather Woodhaven** earned her pilot's license, rode a hot-air balloon over the safari lands of Kenya, parasailed over Caribbean seas, lived through an accidental detour onto a black-diamond ski trail in Aspen and snorkeled among stingrays before becoming a mother of three and wife of one. She channels her love for adventure into writing characters who find themselves in extraordinary circumstances.

### Books by Heather Woodhaven

### Love Inspired Suspense

*Calculated Risk*
*Surviving the Storm*
*Code of Silence*
*Countdown*
*Texas Takedown*
*Tracking Secrets*

# TRACKING
# SECRETS

## HEATHER
## WOODHAVEN

**♦ HARLEQUIN®** LOVE INSPIRED® SUSPENSE

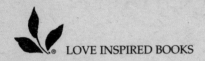 LOVE INSPIRED BOOKS

Recycling programs
for this product may
not exist in your area.

ISBN-13: 978-0-373-45720-5

Tracking Secrets

Copyright © 2017 by Heather Humrichouse

www.Harlequin.com

**Printed in U.S.A.**

Being confident of this very thing,
that He which hath begun a good work in you
will perform it until the day of Jesus Christ.
*–Philippians* 1:6

To Heath, Christina, Justin and Kaitlin.
You know what you did.

# ONE

Nick Kendrick lifted the edge of his shirt to wipe the sweat from his eyes. He needed to run only a little farther before starting his cooldown. A creek to his left rushed over boulders. The birds chirped and trees rustled in the breeze.

Despite his struggle to get started, the exertion loosened his neck and back muscles after a long day of treating animals and appeasing their owners. The trails south of Barings, Idaho, were a treat for the senses. He could leave all the stress behind.

A black Labrador rounded the corner, followed by a woman. Her brown hair, highlighted by the sun, blew back in waves. Unlike him in his sloppy basketball shorts and gray T-shirt, she looked as if she had just stepped out of a corporate meeting. A peach button-down blouse and matching pleated skirt ended just past her knees. Her sparkly sandals reflected the sunlight streaming through the trees.

While pretty, it wasn't exactly the most practical apparel for hiking the trail on the outskirts of town. The black Lab by her side looked to be a little over a year old, maybe two. If he had to guess, the dog still had to gain a good ten pounds before it'd be considered full-grown.

The lady's wide eyes regarded him. Perhaps she was a client, as he was the only veterinarian in the area. If he got closer, he might recognize the dog, which could jar his memory. He'd been so inundated with meeting new people the past several months that he was failing to recall their names.

She frowned and slid her hand into a pocket hidden by the folds in her skirt. If she carried pepper spray, or worse, he didn't want to do anything to startle her. He moved as far right as the trail would allow.

The dog stiffened, and the little hairs on the back of its neck sprung up like a Mohawk hairstyle. Nick followed the dog's gaze behind him but couldn't see anything past the barbed wire fence except aspens and cottonwood trees. He wasn't positive, but he thought the property bumped up against his own.

Was barbed wire really necessary around the residential property? The first wire started two feet off the ground—unless there was another hidden by the tall grass and weeds—followed by two more lines roughly a foot apart.

A rustle in the trees triggered an electric feeling in Nick's spine, and he came to an abrupt stop. A patch of brown moved. A squirrel camouflaged within the matted leaves between the trees wagged its tail.

The dog shot past him, darting underneath the fence. The woman cried out, holding a leash with a collar dangling from its clip. Nick narrowed his gaze and suppressed a groan. Didn't she know better than to walk a dog with a breakaway collar?

"Dog!" she hollered. "Come back!" She ran past

him toward the fence and placed a hand over her mouth at the sight of the barbed wire.

"I'll help you get him." The words were out of his mouth before he could process what that would mean. How would he get over the barbed wire?

"I think it's a her."

His jaw dropped. "You think? You aren't sure?" He cleared his throat and tried to focus on the task at hand. He couldn't afford to get a bad reputation in a small town, but people really shouldn't own dogs without at least some knowledge of how to take care of them properly.

Unless he was willing to slide through on his belly, which he wasn't, the options for getting past the fence were limited. He put one foot on the bottom line to lower it as far as possible. He slipped off the other sneaker and used it like a glove to lift the upper line.

The woman didn't hesitate and stepped through the space. The edge of her skirt caught on one of the barbs, forming a string that now hung down past the hem. She groaned. "I wore the wrong clothing for this. It was supposed to be a nice stroll. Dog!" she hollered again.

"It might help if you called her by her name."

She ignored him and gingerly took his sneaker from his hand so she could mirror his method of holding the barbed wire apart. "Your turn," she said. "Maybe we should call the police. I'm a little worried the owners won't take kindly to intruders if they have a barbed wire fence."

"I'm pretty certain they won't mind if we're merely trying to get a dog off their land." He bent over to step through the space then slipped his shoe back on. It would also give him an excuse to introduce himself to them. If his neighbors knew something he didn't, maybe he needed to invest in an upgrade of his own fence. He scanned the land and spotted movement ahead. The dog had slowed near a house barely visible through the thick grove of trees. He quickened his pace back to a jog.

"Speaking of names, I'm Nick Kendrick."

She raised her eyebrows and pumped her arms alongside him. "That rhymes. I'm Alexis."

Nick couldn't help but notice she didn't offer a last name. "And you don't know your dog's name?" He tried to keep the frustration from his voice.

"No, I do…" She inhaled but focused on her footing. The sandals were strapped on but couldn't be very comfortable for running through a forest. "I think it's… Raven. Yeah. I'm pretty sure that's her name. And it's not my dog. I'm temping for a pet-sitting service."

Her hands moved to emphasize each sentence. "I said I'd never pet sit, but I let my friend twist my arm since it's a holiday weekend. I'm worried the dog won't come back to me. She doesn't know me. I was supposed to take her for a forty-five minute walk. That's it."

Nick's indignation slipped away. It was the pet-sitting company's fault for not having enough staff on Labor Day weekend. They'd obviously sent her without training. The name Raven sounded familiar, though. He pointed at the leash in Alexis's hand and the empty collar hanging from it. "That's a safety collar. They're great for during the day in case they catch themselves on something but not so great for walking and squirrel-gazing."

She rolled her eyes. "Well, someone could've told me that."

They burst through the last row of trees into the clearing. A Tudor-style house with a steeply pitched roof and a half-timbered frame sat in the center. Raven had lost the race with the squirrel and seemed intent on something else. The dog ran around the house, jumped up onto the gutter downspout at the corner and feverishly scratched at it.

"Oh, great. No! Dog, no," Alexis shouted. "That's the last thing I need. I'm not an official contractor with the company. If she damages the house, I'm probably liable. Why do I let myself get talked into these things?" She spoke at speeds that could rival auctioneers or impassioned lawyers.

The dog hopped down and shoved its nose as far as it could go inside the end of the gutter before it sat, almost as if at attention. Had the squirrel run up the gutter? Raven wagged her tail, looked back at them and then caught another sniff. She raced to the other end of the house and jumped on the corresponding downspout, repeating the entire routine. "An odd thing to do twice," he commented.

With Raven's full attention on the gutter, it was their best chance to get her. Nick sprinted ahead at top speed, hoping he wouldn't scare her away. The dog looked up but seemed to grin at his fast approach. Nick smiled back. "Good girl."

She wagged in response. Nick dropped to a knee and put one hand on the loose skin behind her ears so he could grab her if need be. "I'll take that leash now," he called out. The dog lurched forward, shoving her nose into the gutter again. A rustle of plastic caught Nick's attention. "What do you see, girl?" He bent over. A plastic package filled with white powder peeked out. His stomach sank, and he prayed it wasn't what it appeared to be.

Raven sat, and Nick spotted a white patch on her chest that looked like a heart. It jogged his memory. Of course, she was the new drug dog in detection training. He'd performed a physical and administered vaccinations right after her owner—a name that escaped him—adopted her a few months ago. But that meant Raven thought she was working. His heart rate sped up.

Alexis slid a little on the leaves as she came to a stop. "Here's the collar." She dangled it, still attached to the leash, as he straightened. "Is there a problem?" she asked.

He didn't know how to answer that. He removed the breakaway collar and looped the leash around Raven's neck to make sure she couldn't escape again in the event she caught the scent of another squirrel. Nick stood, the end of the leash in hand. The dog took off in front of him, heading back for the first gutter.

Nick let her lead. Raven shoved her nose in the gutter before she sat, wagging her tail. He took a knee and bent over to see what was in there. The same telltale bag was squished inside. If it was what he thought it was, they needed to get off the property fast. He hoped this property had a better cell signal than his did. "We need to call the—"

Something crunched.

Brown work boots rounded the corner. Nick flung

his hands to his own shoe closest to the gutter as if he were tying the shoelaces. He looked up into the eyes of a burly middle-aged man and attempted a smile. "Hi. Shoe untied."

The man's eyes narrowed, but he said nothing. It didn't take a genius to realize this was not normal neighbor behavior.

Nick straightened to standing but didn't take his gaze off the man. He could hear Alexis approach, so he began walking backward in hopes she'd get the hint. "Sorry to intrude," he said. "As you can see, our dog took off after a squirrel, and we had to catch her. Had a collar issue, but it's fixed now. One-time issue. You won't be seeing us again. We'll be going."

Alexis entered his peripheral vision. She tilted her head and gave him an odd look. The man raised his phone to waist level. His right thumb was busy moving. Awareness hit Nick in the gut.

Either the guy thought they were trying to steal his drugs, or the man was a scout for the real traffickers. Both options meant they were in serious trouble.

"It's my fault we're on your property," Alexis said. She took a step forward with her hand outstretched. "I'm—"

"Honey," Nick blurted. He couldn't let her reveal her name and become marked.

She whirled around on the spot, her dark brown eyes wild with indignation. Her forehead creased and smoothed in an instant. She pursed her lips, tilted her head and studied his face as if searching for a reason for his sudden change in behavior.

He reached out with the hand that didn't have a

leash and grabbed her wrist. She frowned but didn't try to pull away or argue.

"We've taken enough of this man's time," he said. "We need to finish our jog." Nick glanced at the way Alexis was dressed and knew that was the wrong thing to say. "More of a fast walk, really. Our friends are waiting back on the path." He chanced a glance at the man's hard eyes. "We're visiting, and they're eager to take us to the shooting range." Okay, the last part might've been a bit too much because it was obvious they didn't have guns on their persons. But he wanted to make it clear to the man they weren't going down without a fight.

The sound of tires spraying gravel echoed through the trees. A vehicle was approaching at high speed. Not good.

The man straightened his torso so he looked even taller. "How about you meet *my* friends first?"

The coldness of his voice chilled Nick's bones, and he knew the vehicle fast approaching wouldn't be filled with friendly neighbors. He lifted his chin to the right. "You mean them?"

The man turned his head. Nick didn't wait for him to realize the vehicle hadn't arrived yet. He pulled on Alexis's arm and yanked her around the corner of the house. She tugged her arm free but ran with him and Raven without any discussion.

A truck squealed to a stop. Nick picked a path around the thickest grouping of trees, choosing the biggest ones in hopes they'd obscure the view of the men who started yelling at each other behind them. The man's *friends* had arrived.

He couldn't make out much of what they said except two words: "Get them."

A gunshot rang out. Alexis ducked and put both hands over her head. A scream tore from her throat. The dog answered with a bark. The bullet snapped a branch, which spun and smacked the side of her neck.

She fought against confusion. For some reason men were shooting at them and she'd just helped give away their location. She hadn't meant to scream, but she'd never been shot at before.

Nick grabbed her upper arm again and pulled her around another tree. He kept his fingers there, tugging, silently urging her to run faster, but her sandals didn't have much grip. It was all she could do to keep up without falling on her face.

Alexis fought a surge of nausea as several men's voices filtered through the trees. "Use the jammer," one shouted. They were trying to make sure she and Nick couldn't call for help.

"Shoot only on sight. We don't need the whole valley showing up!" It sounded like the voice of the man who had confronted them at the house, but she couldn't be sure. Why were these men so angry they'd stepped onto the property? It didn't make sense.

Maybe they'd recognized Nick and had a score to settle with him. What kind of man had she aligned herself with? Maybe Nick had seen something she hadn't. It seemed too late to point out to the men with guns that she wasn't a threat to them.

Tires squealed and covered up whatever else the man yelling had to say. She couldn't afford to slow down to dial 911 on her cell phone, but she had an uneasy feeling that it wouldn't work anyway.

She stumbled over a rock, and Nick's fingers slipped off her arm. She managed to fall forward in a sloppy run but regained her balance. Nick's golden eyes met hers for half a second before he motioned with his head which direction they needed to go. He took off without waiting for her agreement.

That was the opposite direction of where she wanted to go. Instead of heading for the path near the river, he was taking her through the trees and, in a roundabout way, back toward the front of the house. Though if they could reach the road unseen, maybe they had a better chance of escape.

There were rarely cars on the outskirts of town, so she couldn't count on waving someone down for help. The area was mountainous, and the only reasons anyone would come out here were that they owned property or were heading for the trail.

Nick gave the leash a quick tug, and the dog stayed right at his side. She followed them around a full-grown blue spruce with spider webs running over sections of the branches. He held up a finger. Her bare calves brushed up against a prickly branch, and she cringed but didn't move.

Stepping past her, Nick peeked around the tree, and then pivoted back toward her. He grabbed her hand and shoved her farther into the prickly foliage. She resisted slightly, not so much because of the uncomfortable pine needles but more because of the potential of spiders.

For a second it looked as if Nick wanted to give her a high-five, but he swung his hand in an arc at his side.

Raven flopped down as if she was bored, though she kept her eyes on Nick. Alexis was impressed at his use of the silent command, but the crunching sound of tires nearby flung the thoughts away.

She slipped her hand into her pocket and, using tiny movements, fished her phone out. The slash through the image of the cell tower on the screen confirmed her fear. No help would be coming. They were alone.

A motor roared. She turned her head slightly, hoping she wasn't drawing attention to herself. A white pickup truck vaulted through the trees, breaking branches left and right. Her breath hitched at the sight of men carrying assault rifles. They flanked the truck in a V shape as they marched south toward the trail and the river.

She remained frozen, her back protesting from the strain of a typical office workday. She was very aware of Nick pressed against her, especially after she lost sight of the men with guns. His face was a nice oval shape with kind eyes and a full mouth. His hair was a light brown, flared up at the crown, either from running in the wind or hair gel. He was slightly taller than she was, so probably close to five foot ten, and he obviously stayed fit.

It felt like hours passed, but the sun's blinding glare from the west never changed, so it had likely been mere minutes. The beams filtered through the tree branches, making it hard to see if the men were truly gone.

Her heart rate sped, and her stomach churned. Her breathing remained erratic, but Nick stood as still as a statue. Maybe he was used to running from guns.

"The scout is still at the house," Nick whispered

into her ear. His breath smelled like Junior Mints, a fact she tried to ignore. "There might be others waiting there, as well. Stay quiet and follow me."

She wanted to ask what he meant by "the scout" but didn't trust herself to open her mouth without being too loud. Her mom had always told her she didn't know how to whisper properly. It's why she'd always chosen to pass notes rather than confer in law proceedings.

He seemed to be waiting for a response. She nodded her agreement. He squeezed her wrist in reply and gave it a small tug. They darted around the next tree. Nick froze again. Her ears strained to hear signs of someone close by before moving on.

The pattern continued until Alexis felt certain they must be nearing the road. Instead they came to a fence. Nick audibly sighed. He took off his shoe and handed it to her in a wordless request to hold the barbed wire fence the way she had when they'd followed Raven's dash for a squirrel.

This is what she got for not following her instincts. Theresa knew that she would temp anywhere except the pet-sitting company. But Alexis loved Theresa. The woman had become as close as any friend she'd had, despite technically being Alexis's boss. And when Theresa had called, her voice had sounded deliriously happy.

"Please, Alexis. You know I'd never ask you to do this if I wasn't in a bind. If you can't, I'll come back early, but the thing is…" Theresa's voice had dropped to a whisper. "I'm seeing someone. And we're already out of town on a weekend together. I know what you're going to say, and don't worry. We're in separate rooms, but honey, I've known him all my life, and I think he could be the one."

"Who?" Alexis had pressed.

"I can't tell you yet. I promised him we'd keep it hush-hush. He doesn't want us to have the pressure of being under a microscope. You know how small towns can be."

She *did* know how small towns could be, but in the last year she'd heard no evidence of the rumor mill. Perhaps because she kept to herself since she'd moved back.

Nick stepped through the barbed wire fence first. Alexis looked over her shoulder. Nick must have chosen this section of the fence to cross since the trees were especially thick here. Raven didn't seem so keen to slide underneath the fence this time.

"Hand her to me," he whispered.

Alexis cringed. If the dog so much as licked her, it would have to fend for itself. She exhaled and put her arms around the dog's torso. Her biceps and lower back strained with the effort. The dog had to be at least fifty pounds!

If she hadn't been such a pushover she would've told Theresa no. Then Theresa would've been forced to skip her weekend to walk the dog, probably on the sidewalks of downtown instead of the trail, and none of this would've ever happened.

Nick reached over the fence and took Raven from her. She'd never seen the man around town, which was unusual. He was either new in town or they ran in completely different circles. It made her question again whether she should've trusted him enough to follow him, but she didn't have much choice now. He had the dog.

He held the fence open for her, and she stepped through. Her outfit, now covered with black dog hair and smudges of nature, would never recover, but it was a small price to pay for getting back to safety. The list of charges she wanted to report against those men ran through her head on a loop.

Nick gathered the leash tightly and waved for her to follow him as he broke into a fast-paced jog. Her feet felt every rock and hard patch of uneven ground through the thin soles of her shoes. If she ever got home, she'd never wear the sandals again.

Five minutes later, the trees opened up into a pasture. The tall grass swayed with the breeze, and in the distance, a yellow house with white shutters looked welcoming. A red barn stood behind it. Two horses grazed nearby.

She marveled at the perfect picture of tranquility. It belonged on a postcard and made her long for her own pair of cowboy boots. "Do you know the owners?"

"The owner. Yes," he answered.

They approached another fence, this one made from wooden rails. The large spaces made it easy to slip through. Even though the wood couldn't protect her, the physical barrier made her heart slow ever so slightly. "I'll feel a lot safer once we're inside that house. I hope someone's home."

He pulled a phone out of his pocket and dialed. "We need to find a signal now. I don't think those jammers can cover that large a distance." He ran a few steps. "Weak," he muttered. His eyebrows rose. "Dial tone."

He pressed a few numbers and held it up to his ear. "We need help."

Alexis put a hand on her racing heart and issued a silent prayer of thanks that he'd been able to reach the authorities. Their pace didn't slow as Nick spoke feverishly about men with guns and rattled off an address Alexis didn't recognize.

"Please hurry." Nick swiveled the cell phone so the microphone rested on his shoulder. "They want me to stay on the line until they get here."

He looked over her shoulder, and she followed his gaze. The property appeared to be roughly five acres until a line of trees obscured the rest. She imagined that just past it was the walking path and the river. "Is that them?"

The sound of cracking branches in the distance made her flinch.

"Follow me." They sprinted until they reached the porch of the house. He lifted the phone to his ear. "It sounds like they've made it to the trail behind my property. I have to put the phone down now. Please hurry."

*His* property? He pulled a set of keys out of his pocket and opened the navy blue door. Past the darkened hallway, bright sunshine streamed through a wall of windows. A rifle suddenly blocked her view, taking her breath away.

Nick held one in each hand. "I hope you know how to shoot a gun."

# TWO

Nick reached back into the gun safe hidden within his front closet to grab ammunition. He had only a couple of guns just in case wolves attacked his horses. When he first acquired the property, the previous owner said it'd be a good precaution. So far, there hadn't been any need. "Ideally we won't have to use these."

"I've shot a handgun." She held the rifle gingerly with both hands. "Once. A cop I knew was showing me how. I decided it wasn't for me." Her hair looked wild and mussed, and one side of her blouse was no longer tucked into the skirt. "I'd rather hide than try to use this."

He glanced out the window and squinted. The white metal through the trees slowed. If the men in the truck didn't have binoculars, they wouldn't be able to see Alexis and him. But if they did…

"Step into the shadows." He waved at Raven to lie down again, and the dog complied.

The truck didn't make another appearance, but men spilled from the trees onto his property. Maybe barbed wire fences weren't overkill after all. He shoved the ammunition into the rifle and proceeded to load the second rifle for her. "Only as a precaution."

She nodded. "How many times have you shot a gun?"

It probably wouldn't help her anxiety to admit he was no sharpshooter. Sure, he practiced, but only enough to feel safe and competent. It wasn't a hobby or something he considered fun. He'd rather ride a horse or hike in his free time.

"Enough to know what I'm doing," he replied. The thought of having to shoot at a human being made his stomach turn. "You stay here and holler if they reach the wooden fence. I'm going to my office to see if they're approaching from the side."

For a second he thought she'd refuse, but she inhaled and took a knee at the corner of the hallway and the living room. Raven lay down and rested her head against Alexis, who flinched and stared at the dog warily but didn't move away.

He wondered what her story was, because there were few people in the world who could resist the charms of such a sweet Labrador. But then again, he couldn't judge her true personality when they'd just had to run away from gunmen.

He strode down the hall and lifted the window just enough that he could slip the barrel of the gun outside to aim. He closed his eyes a half second. "Please, Lord," he whispered, "defend us."

The dog howled, a mournful song with vibrato.

"Nick, how do I get her to stop?" Alexis cried out. "They're going to know we're here for sure if she keeps this up."

He ran back to them. Raven remained on the

ground but pointed her nose in the air as she released another song. Odd unless... He strained his ears. "Listen."

Alexis dropped the rifle and stood up, a gorgeous smile on her face. "The police. Help is coming." She looked over her shoulder to the window. Men were running back into the trees. "They hear it, too." She placed a hand on his arm. "Thank you for getting us somewhere safe."

The rifle rested at his side. He was relieved, as well, but the danger had been too close, too real. His chest hurt from either breathing too hard or the fight to keep his heart from jumping out of his chest.

His mom had already received one sorrowful call too many. It would've destroyed her to be told her remaining son was also killed by drug dealers.

His brother, an undercover federal agent, had been killed by the drug runners he had tried to expose. Nick wouldn't allow his brother's death to be in vain, and while it didn't make sense for him to abandon his veterinary training and take his brother's place in the DEA, he could step up and lead. The memory of his brother had driven Nick to develop an interest in politics.

In his opinion, the current elected officials weren't doing all they could to diminish the impact of living in what the government had deemed a High Intensity Drug Trafficking Area. No one wanted to acknowledge the label, but living right alongside a major interstate meant they needed to face facts. Which was why he was running for mayor in the upcoming election.

The sirens grew closer. Alexis glanced back and forth between the view of the backyard and the front window. Raven stopped her soulful song but looked at Nick with expectation. He opened the front door in time to see two police cars pull to a stop in his circular drive.

He set the rifle against the doorway before he ran down the stairs to greet them. Four officers jumped out of the two vehicles. They all seemed to have eyes only for Alexis. Nick still hadn't gotten used to feeling like the outsider in the town where he'd lived for over a year now.

"They are driving on the hiking trail just past the trees," Alexis shouted as she stepped beside him. "If you hurry you can get them."

While he'd never seen vehicles on the trail before, it was wide enough to accommodate horses, bikes and runners, and if the cops didn't hurry, the men would be able to drive all the way to the parking lot at the trailhead. Once there, they could hit the road that went into town or take the interstate and disappear.

The older policeman who seemed to be in charge pointed a finger at the men in front of him. Two officers jumped into the first cruiser and took off. The remaining officer looked significantly younger, as if he was fresh out of high school.

"Chief Spencer," Alexis said, "I didn't get a chance to tell them it was a white pickup truck."

The chief frowned. "Is that all you can tell me?"

She crossed her arms. "I'm sorry I didn't get a better look while they were shooting at me." She emphasized the last three words. "It's something to go on, right?"

Nick racked his brain to think of another defining

detail he could offer, but she had a point. They didn't take time to look as they focused on staying alive.

Chief Spencer shook his head. "Over half the town owns pickup trucks, Lexi, and a quarter of those are white, including mine."

Nick couldn't help but notice Alexis's grimace when the chief called her Lexi. Her nickname? "He's right," Nick admitted. "I've got a white pickup, too."

The young cop nodded. "Easiest color to keep clean."

"You all have white trucks?" Alexis asked, sounding more incredulous. "Well, I think it was a Ford F-Series." She raised her eyebrows as if they should be impressed.

Nick didn't recall the make and model, so he acknowledged her keen observation with a slow nod.

"That narrows it down to maybe sixty percent of the white trucks," the chief said. Alexis seemed crestfallen, but the chief paid no attention. He looked at Nick. "You said the shooting started at the mayor's house?"

Nick frowned. "Mayor Simonds is my neighbor?" That seemed like a tidbit someone could've mentioned before now. The houses were several acres apart, but still. "I've tried to introduce myself a few times, but no one has ever been home."

The chief narrowed his eyes. "Yes, he is. And I believe you're his opponent, Dr. Kendrick, so if you don't mind, I'd like an impartial party to tell the story." He turned his gaze to Alexis.

Her mouth dropped open. "You're running for mayor? Have you even lived here long enough to be a resident?"

Her tone sounded almost accusatory, and he didn't really understand why. "I've met all the eligibility requirements, if that's what you're asking. Barings is my home."

"Everyone knows he's running, Lexi," the young officer said to Alexis. "Old news."

Her eyebrows shot up, and she eyed him a minute before turning to Chief Spencer. She relayed the events of the past hour without commentary, as if reporting for the six o'clock news. Nick did his best to keep his mouth shut until she reached the part about the man who'd walked around the corner. "Six feet tall, I'd guess," she said. "Late thirties or early forties. He wore a white polo shirt and carpenter jeans. No other identifying factors that I can remember."

"There were drugs," Nick interjected. "In the gutter downspouts. I can show you."

Alexis's jaw dropped. Chief noticed. "You didn't see these drugs?"

She cringed. "No, but it certainly explains a lot. I can't think of any other motivation they'd try to kill us just for getting a dog off the property."

Chief Spencer shook his head again. "I need a reason to get on that property. And frankly, having the mayor's opponent as the only witness doesn't do it."

"Forget that, then," Alexis said. "We're talking attempted murder. I was witness to that! Those men shot a branch that hit me." She lifted up her hair. An angry red line streaked across the side of her neck.

Nick flinched. He should've moved faster, gotten them out of the line of fire before that had happened. He turned to enter the house. "I'll grab my first aid kit."

Her hand blocked him. "I'm fine. It just stings a little." Her gaze swung to the chief. "My point is, I don't understand why you don't have enough to go on."

The younger officer picked up his radio and stepped away for a moment. "Chief, no sign of the vehicle or armed men. They confirmed tire tracks and a broken fence section on the mayor's property. Permission to proceed?"

Nick tensed. He wasn't used to having his word questioned. Was that how every officer would react if a challenging political opponent witnessed criminal activity? Or was it possible the chief was proving his alliance with the current mayor? Either way, Nick breathed easier knowing they couldn't avoid the proof that something had happened.

Chief Spencer pointed to the backseat of the vehicle. "Okay. Get in, you two."

Alexis couldn't believe they had to share the backseat of a police vehicle with a dog. Logically, she knew it wouldn't attack her, but the positive thoughts did nothing to stop her heart from racing. Why people liked to keep animals around for company was beyond the scope of her imagination. If they knew what it felt like to be attacked by one like she did, maybe they'd feel differently. The dog's breath alone was enough to make her want to go running. And yet, even though Alexis had shown her no signs of affection, Raven stared up at her, panting.

"She knows you don't like her," Nick said. "Animals can sense that, especially dogs. She's trying to win you over."

She eyed Nick. The chief had referred to him as Dr.

Kendrick. Judging by his tan skin and athletic physique, he had to be active and a lover of the outdoors. And it seemed like those types often loved dogs just as much as nature, so maybe he knew something about animals. "So if I pet her, she'll leave me alone?"

He shrugged. "Wouldn't hurt to try."

She held back a sigh. She'd already touched the dog more than enough for her lifetime when she had to pick it up to get it over the fence, but she humored the both of them and reached out to touch the top of Raven's head. It was smooth yet wiry.

Raven stretched her neck at the touch so that Alexis's fingers brushed against her ears. They were soft and velvety like a fuzzy pillow. The dog shifted in the small space between her and Nick until its whole body leaned against Alexis.

Admittedly, the warmth and connection were nice for a second, but she still didn't trust the dog to keep its mouth to itself. She shot Nick a look.

He smirked. "Or petting her could just encourage her."

Her gut twisted. She knew he was teasing, but she didn't know him well enough to explain why it wasn't funny. Alexis pushed away from the dog, calmly, forcing it to snuggle with Nick instead.

How could he have lived here long enough to be running for mayor? She'd thought she knew the few doctors who lived in the area. She'd worked for almost all of them, subbing for their receptionists.

She'd kept to herself ever since she returned to town, but she must have been more antisocial than she'd thought if Jeremy, the young officer driving, was right and his candidacy was old news.

Nick patted the dog's head and her tail wagged, slapping Alexis's thigh. Nick's warm laugh soothed her nerves. "Sorry about that," he said.

She tried to smile in response.

Jeremy parked the cruiser in front of the mayor's house. She'd known Gerald Simonds lived out here somewhere but hadn't known which house until now. He was only a few years older. She'd never imagined him as rich or running their town, but he owned a successful mechanic shop and had made some smart investment moves. In fact, his brother, Barry, owned the financial firm responsible. Barry used to do only bookkeeping, but everyone, it seemed, including her parents, had wanted to sign on with Barry as their financial advisor after seeing Gerald's success.

Officer Jeremy Wicks opened the door for her. She had over ten years on him. Most days, she still considered herself young. She'd crossed the thirty-year mark, but she could remember changing Jeremy's diapers when she worked as a mother's helper one summer. He'd been an officer for a little over a year, but it was still weird seeing him with a gun and handcuffs.

He nodded at her. "Ma'am."

She fought back a groan and hustled around the car. While she hated when people used her childhood nickname of Lexi, she hated even more when they called her *ma'am*. She was still a *Miss* until she got married, in her mind.

Some days she wondered if she had missed out on her chance for marriage by going after her career and law school with such singular focus. Her head had spent so much of the time stuck in the pages of law statutes that she'd forgotten how to flirt. Maybe she had never known how in the first place.

There weren't many attractive, employed, witty men in Barings. The few that existed had already been taken. She'd pegged Nick for a nice guy as soon as he'd offered to help her get Raven. That is, until she found out he had political ambitions. Now she realized he had to be either a naive idealist or power hungry. At least, that had been her experience with political science majors back in school.

Maybe she was wrong and Nick was the nice guy she'd first imagined. But if he was, she should keep her distance. Her past would prove a problem for his dreams.

Nick led the dog back around the gutters. Raven stuck her nose in both, but when Jeremy leaned down in front of each of them, he shook his head. "Nothing, sir," he said to the chief.

"Can't you do a drug residue test?" Nick asked.

"Here's the thing." The chief tilted his head to the side. "I can come on this property because I had reason to suspect I'd find some gunmen. We haven't. I can look at the gutters because they're on the outside of the house. If contraband is in plain sight, it's fair game, but I don't have enough probable cause to perform a residue test."

"But I saw the drugs," Nick said.

He nodded toward Alexis. "And if Lexi had seen them, too, then we'd be in business."

Alexis shifted her gaze away from Nick. She felt bad enough that she'd put him in the situation in the first place. He'd saved her life and the dog's, for that matter. She wished she had seen the drugs, but she couldn't bring herself to lie.

"What about the dog?" Nick's demeanor brightened. "I can't verify without my records, but I think this is the K9 detection dog I examined several months back."

"Wait," Alexis said. "You examined her? You're a veterinarian?" The questions came out accusatory. The information had just taken her by surprise. She hadn't imagined he would be a doctor of animals. Well, that ruled out another eligible bachelor. Even if he ended up losing the mayoral election, they could never have a future because as a vet, he probably wanted to own a dog, if he didn't already. And that was a deal breaker. Why did all the great guys love dogs?

Jeremy raised an eyebrow. "You need to get out more, Lexi." He stepped forward. "So is this Raven? Joe's dog?" He dropped to a knee and looked at Alexis. "They left you to take care of her?"

He could've skipped the incredulous tone. Though it was no secret in the town that she wasn't exactly fond of dogs. One notch short of terrified, really. "It was a favor for Theresa. Theresa said if she didn't get someone to take care of her right away, she'd have to come back tonight to do the job personally."

Jeremy took the leash from Nick and ruffled Raven's ears. The dog responded by nuzzling into him.

The chief folded his arms over his sizable chest and studied the dog. "This is Raven, huh? Joe's technically retired from the force but trains K9 dogs all over the country. You know, he was training this dog for us. She was going to be his last one. He planned to gift her to our department."

Jeremy shook his head but kept his gaze on the dog. "Last I heard he was in critical condition." He straightened and handed the leash to Alexis.

"Critical?" Alexis asked.

Chief nodded. "Hit-and-run just last night. Raven was in her harness and did fine, but Joe had to be air-lifted a few hours away to Boise."

That explained the sudden need for someone to watch the dog.

Nick's frown deepened. "Well, if she's a drug detection dog, you should have cause to test for residue."

Chief shook his head. "I know for a fact Raven's not certified yet. Last I knew, Joe said she had a heap of potential but some obedience issues. She hasn't been in the program long enough for testing. Takes a minimum of a year, from what I understand. Besides, didn't you say you were on this property because she broke off the leash in pursuit of a squirrel?"

Alexis felt her cheeks heat but knew that the chief was right. If Raven wasn't certified and court-qualified, her skills would be inadmissible in court. Not that they needed or wanted her opinion.

Chief sighed. "I'm sorry, but I can't hunt down a judge and an out-of-town mayor on a holiday week-end for this." He gestured to the downspouts. "Let's say you're right. For all we know, this was a dead drop gone wrong, so it doesn't do me any good to search the mayor's house. He's visiting family."

In other words, the chief didn't want to risk bad publicity. She'd read the news headlines. A mayor in

Maine had been an unwitting victim of a dead drop. The drug runners would send packages of drugs to addresses that likely wouldn't answer the door. The mayor in Maine sued the police department after they'd raided his home, scaring his wife and children.

Nick's eyes implored Alexis. "Did you recognize any of the men?"

"From town? No, but I haven't been that observant lately. I didn't recognize you." She sighed. "I'd guess the man who talked to us was in his early forties. The men with guns…" She strained to remember any important details and failed. "Everything was a blur once shots were fired."

"I think the guy we talked to was a scout," Nick added.

"You said that before. What was he scouting for?" Alexis questioned.

Jeremy looked like he was struggling not to roll his eyes. "They serve as guides for drug shipments. They aren't the actual ones to pick them up. They go ahead and make sure the coast is clear. Oftentimes they don't have weapons or drugs on their person, so if they get picked up, we've got nothing on them."

"They serve as both spies and decoys?"

Nick looked at her, as if impressed. "Basically."

"If Lexi thinks they're not from here, it's unlikely they've made the two of you targets," the chief mused.

She wasn't so sure they should rely on her knowledge of residents. She hadn't recognized Nick as being from the area, either, though he claimed he'd been here the past year. He was running for mayor, after all. She knew she'd been closed off, but this seemed like a wake-up call. The past year she'd been downright antisocial with her head stuck in the sand.

"I made sure they didn't get our names," Nick added.

"That was quick thinking," she admitted. Her neck grew hot as she remembered how it felt to have him speak so tenderly when he called her *honey*. Now Nick smiled at her, which didn't help. She knew from experience that her neck probably was beet red at the moment.

Chief nodded. "Good. Here's what we're going to do. My boys are going to walk the property and see if we have anything to go on. I'll set up a patrol car to drive by your houses tonight. We'll keep a watch out for any trucks that look suspicious." His radio chirped. "We're going to be combing the area now. We'll give you a quick ride back to your place and take it from there."

"What about Nick? They know where he lives."

Chief shrugged. "Not necessarily. They just saw you run to the neighboring property."

Alexis tightened her hold on the leash. His words didn't comfort her.

She replayed the events of the evening on a loop, searching for something that could help. There'd been a click. She was sure of it. "What I don't understand is, if scouts are just making sure the coast is clear, then why did he take our picture?"

Nick spun around, a look of alarm on his face. "Are you sure?"

"I think…" She looked up at the clouds, trying to picture it. "He had his phone in his hand while you were talking to him." She nodded. "His thumb moved, and the phone clicked when I stepped toward him to introduce myself. That's when you stopped me. What else could the click have been?"

"Let's not jump to conclusions just yet," the chief said.

Nick's face took on an ashen tone as he closed his eyes. "We've been marked."

# THREE

Only a few hours ago, Nick had been looking forward to a quiet long weekend at home. Now he was on a drug ring's most-wanted list.

"What do you mean marked?" Alexis stepped in front of him. Her intense gaze demanded his attention.

"It means they'll take us out if they think we are going to cause them problems." He gestured out at the town, north of them. "It means that every member in their cartel likely has our photo. It means we need to watch our backs."

Chief put his hand on Alexis's shoulder. "We don't know that for sure. Let's just take it one step at a time." He led her to the backseat of the cruiser, but not before he leveled a disapproving glare at Nick.

Nick didn't regret what he'd said, though. Not knowing the full truth wouldn't help Alexis stay safe. Ever since his brother had died, Nick had found out everything he could about drug trafficking, specifically in the Northwest. It wasn't something to be taken lightly. The cartels had sophisticated ways of communicating, and the intel they shared with each other rivaled that of most three-letter government agencies.

Nick called Raven into the car and took his seat. Alexis scrunched her nose. "Didn't you hear the click from his phone, too? Maybe I imagined it."

The hopefulness in her voice was difficult to ignore. "It was hard enough to think straight with blood rushing to my head. Don't second-guess yourself, even though we'd both love it if you were wrong."

She stared ahead, her face pale. It took only a minute to arrive back at his place.

"Where'd you park?" the young officer asked her.

"The lot at the trailhead. Could you take me there, Jeremy? I'd really rather not walk back alone, if that's okay."

"Understandable." Jeremy nodded. "You still driving that bucket of bolts you call a car?"

She lifted her chin. "Hey. A little respect. It's a classic."

"Dream on." Jeremy shook his head. "Never seen a lawyer drive such a crummy car before."

Nick's neck tingled, and he couldn't place his finger on why. If he hadn't known better, he'd have wondered if he was jealous that the young cop talked to Alexis in such a friendly manner. "You're a lawyer?" he asked her. "I'd tell you a lawyer joke, but—"

"—you're afraid you'd get sued," she said. Her face reddened, and she pressed her lips together in a firm line. "Trust me, I've heard them all. Besides, I wasn't that kind of lawyer."

A crackly voice came over the radio. "Possible domestic disturbance called in. Shouting heard next to the burned-out barn on Garrett property."

The dispatcher's description was yet another reminder that Nick wasn't in the big city anymore. The chief shook his head. "We need to get this."

The car pulled to a stop. "I'll take her to her car," Nick said. They hopped out and the cruiser sped away.

Alexis swung her chin from left to right, her eyes darting every which way.

"If they had come back here already, the cops would've seen them," Nick said gently.

Her shoulders sank. "I hope you're right."

Nick escorted her and the dog to the garage, where he entered the five-digit access code. The cab of his pickup truck had two rows, so he guided Raven into the back instead of next to Alexis. He pointed in the direction of the trail. "It would've taken you a good half hour to get back to the parking lot if you had walked."

"Theresa said the dog needed a forty-five minute walk. I rounded up." She flashed a sheepish grin, and they both got situated in the truck. "I hadn't reached my daily step goal yet, and I needed some time to clear my head."

He started the ignition and pulled out onto the county highway. "It seems common knowledge that you have a love for dogs." He hoped his teasing tone would get her to open up.

She groaned. "Why is it that when people say they don't like cats, it's okay, but disliking dogs is equivalent to hating babies?" Her eyes widened. "Which I don't!"

"Good to know." He smiled in the rearview mirror at Raven, who seemed to be enjoying the conversation. "Dogs make it pretty easy to love them."

"You mean aside from the presents they leave in

the yard, the smell, the drool and the nice things they eat?"

He laughed. "Bad experience?" If she was a lawyer, maybe a dog ate a pair of her expensive shoes.

She stiffened and watched him for a moment, as if considering whether to talk or not. She looked forward. "A rabid dog attacked me when I was little. The scar doesn't hurt, but when I think about the rabies shots…" She let her voice trail off.

The smile fell off his face at the thought. "That should've never happened," he said softly. "I'm sorry." It frustrated him to no end that some pet owners neglected treatment of their animals. A simple vaccine would've prevented the dog's disease and Alexis's pain.

"Not your fault. I'm not scared anymore. I got over it." She nodded with each phrase, as if reciting a script. "They just aren't my favorite."

She pulled her shoulders back and raised her chin. She might have told herself she wasn't scared anymore, but the way she'd flinched when Raven tried to snuggle proved otherwise. It wasn't that she disliked dogs, like she tried to infer, but that she was scared.

The mountains served as a backdrop to the rows of trees on either side of the road. If he kept going, the trees on the right side would be replaced by a rock wall. Just before town, all the trees disappeared and a sharp curve provided a gorgeous viewing point for the valley. An unbidden image of having a picnic there with Alexis while enjoying the scenery popped into his head. He'd been so focused on school and career the past several years that he'd saved relationships for later. He never wanted to start one that would only end up in the pain of a long-distance relationship. He'd done that once in college and vowed never to do it again.

"Later" had finally arrived, but he'd yet to find someone in the small town who he could imagine as more than a friend.

She pointed at the black medical bag in between their seats. "So you're really a vet?"

The question made him laugh. "Why is that so hard to believe?"

She smiled. "I guess it's not. I just didn't think our small town could support more than one."

He made the final turn toward the trailhead. "That's because it can't. I bought the practice from Doc Finn so he could retire. He moved to the Oregon coast when I came here."

Her mouth dropped. "He did? But his office is practically across the street from where I live."

"My office," he corrected her.

She pulled her head back in surprise. "But the logo hasn't changed! Your name isn't on the building."

He held back a laugh. She must have prided herself on keeping up to date with all new residents if this bothered her so much. "Barings Animal Hospital had a nicer ring to it than Dr. Nick Kendrick's Animal Hospital, so I kept it the same."

She shook her head. "I guess I've had tunnel vision."

"Your law practice staying busy?"

She squinted in confusion. "My what?" Her eyebrows rose and she leaned back. "No. I don't practice law anymore. I came back to spend some time with my parents. I've been working for Theresa's temp agency until I figure out my next step."

"Are they ill?"

"Who? My parents? No, they're doing great. They actually retired to Arizona last month. I'm sticking around until I sell their house. After that…" She looked down at her clasped hands. "Well, I guess time will tell."

In other words, she wouldn't be around much longer, so it'd probably be smart to forget the dinner invitation he wanted to extend to her. Now, if she was willing to open up a practice in town that would be another story. He was tempted to ask why she no longer practiced law, but it seemed too soon for what could be a personal question.

The box of Junior Mints he kept in the cup console rattled when he drove over a rock. He spotted her interest. "You want some? I like to have some after work, before I go on a run. It gives me a little extra burst of energy."

She smiled and almost seemed to be fighting a laugh. "What brought you to Barings? Are you from Idaho?"

"No. I was a city boy, but I wanted my practice to be more than just domestic pets. I like variety and enjoy making house calls for cattle and horses. Barings is a long way from Seattle, but I can make the trip home in one day."

It could've been his imagination, but it seemed she paled. "Seattle, huh?" She pointed to the left. "Turn here."

The small, dusty lot sat next to a brown outhouse and a bulletin board covered in trail maps. A beat-up, rusted, baby-blue Honda Accord that had to be circa 1980 sat by its lonesome. He gaped. "I see why your cop friend was surprised."

"Not you, too. The whole town gives me a hard time." She sighed. "No one sees what I see. This beauty has been faithful to me ever since I bought it cheap in high school. It helped me graduate from law school debt-free." She eyed him. "Not an easy feat."

"If it's anything like veterinary school, I agree." His current debt load wasn't as high as that of most members of his graduating class, but it would've taken a ridiculous amount of discipline, planning and an overloaded work schedule to graduate without a bill. Her debt-free status only served to intrigue him more. He wondered if she'd be willing to have dinner together, just as friends. Though he'd have to make it clear he wasn't interested in a relationship. So it'd be wise to let the idea go, especially since she was moving on soon. Besides, she seemed like the type that took a long time to lower her guard.

He pulled to a stop and stared at the bucket of bolts. "Unfortunately your faithful beauty doesn't look like it's going to last much longer. Is it safe?"

"Absolutely!" Her grin faded. "Probably more than we are, if I understood what you said back there. I hate that it takes a court order to get full-time police protection."

"I didn't mean to scare you, but I believe a healthy dose of caution is necessary." He almost offered to give her one of his rifles but stopped short. She'd made it clear she wasn't comfortable with guns. "Keep your eyes open and don't go places alone."

"That's good advice for any woman on any day."

She stepped out of the truck. "I guess I need to get the dog back home." She tugged on the leash, and Raven followed her out of the truck.

The dog turned her head around and flashed Nick a look so pathetic he almost laughed. "Let me know if you need any help with her."

"I think I've asked enough of you today." She gave him an awkward wave. "Sorry I got you into this mess in the first place, Nick. Thanks for helping me."

"My pleasure, Alexis."

"Thompson," she replied. "Alexis Thompson."

Her eyes narrowed as she said it, as if watching him for a reaction. "Nice to meet you, Alexis."

She nodded. "I'll see you around."

He searched for the right words to say more, to ease the fear he saw in her eyes. She moved to close the passenger door, and he leaned over to stop her. "The more I think about it, the more I realize they have no reason to go after us. We aren't going to be any problem to them. It's going to be fine."

The creases in her forehead disappeared as an authentic smile transformed her face. She looked young and energetic and downright beautiful. She closed the door and walked away. As he waited for her to start her car, Nick hoped he had told her the truth. At the very least, he'd drive behind her until she got home, if only to make sure danger didn't follow.

Alexis placed Raven in the backseat of her car before she got herself situated in the driver's seat. She refused to look, but she felt Nick's gaze on her. From what little she'd observed, he seemed like the type of guy who would wait to make sure she got on the road safely.

Her hands shook as she inserted her keys into the ignition. What a day. If she stopped and reflected on it now, she might never get home. Death was something far in the future. When she read her Bible and spent time in prayer, she had peace that when it was her time, she'd be ready. Her throat tightened. But she wasn't ready for it to be time yet. There was so much more in her life she wanted to do, wanted to be.

Fear must have had an unusual effect on her, since she'd practically gushed her life story to Nick in the course of five minutes. Thankfully she hadn't had much experience with being scared to death before, but she was still surprised at her reaction to Nick.

It would be interesting to see if their dangerous game of hide-and-seek would make the *Barings Herald*. She didn't want to tell her parents and cause them worry if it wasn't absolutely necessary. Her mom had struggled with insomnia enough as it was since Alexis had left Seattle.

The engine struggled to turn over. She groaned, and her cheeks heated. She resisted the urge to look at Nick's reaction. The motor gave another hearty try and hummed to life. She let out a breath, shifted into Reverse and drove out of the lot. Her finances couldn't support a car payment at the moment.

While she was grateful that eight years of ramen noodles, part-time jobs, thrift-store clothes and little sleep had allowed her to graduate debt-free, there weren't too many well-paid jobs available for a disbarred lawyer.

Her stomach turned at the thought. It'd been almost a year, and the shame still washed over her like it was yesterday.

She'd chosen patent law as her specialty because she'd known that she couldn't compartmentalize enough to be a defense lawyer. Never in her wildest dreams had she suspected her client would want to unburden himself and tell her the story of how he murdered his partner. He'd practically gloated over the fact no one had found out. Everyone had assumed the partner had taken some money and left the country.

After two weeks of sleepless nights, she thought she'd found a loophole for attorney-client privilege and submitted to the police what he'd told her. The Washington State Bar Association didn't agree with her conclusions. The confession her client had made to her was inadmissible, and the state of Washington issued the verdict that she would no longer be practicing there.

But it did no good to rehash the past continually.

Alexis clicked on the radio to drown out her thoughts. There would be no more processing of the day, or the past, or even Nick until she reached the safety of her bathtub. And she'd most definitely earned scented bubbles. Lots of them.

She focused on the road. The sun dipped below the horizon and outlined the mountains and trees with pastel colors. She pressed the brakes at the stop sign, but it took some extra force on the pedal to get it to slow down. Her car really was on its last leg. The pedal had never felt this mushy before.

She took the left turn to head back into town. Her rearview mirror showed Nick right behind her. Either he had business in town that he hadn't mentioned, or he was following her all the way home. She smiled into the rearview mirror and hated to admit that it felt good to have someone care like that.

Relationship goals had never been part of her five-year plan, but chatting with Nick had unleashed a sudden, intense longing to have someone to share her life. It was probably past time. But what did a disbarred lawyer have to offer?

The terrain began to change. On the right, the road butted against a foothill. The side was covered with chains to help prevent rockslides. To the left, the evergreens blocked a lot of the light. The road changed into curves, taking her down to the heart of Barings.

In a short while, there would be the sharpest curve, a breathtaking viewpoint where you could look over the cliff at the entire valley. If it weren't for Raven, she'd be tempted to pull into the small parking lot to sit and process the last few hours. The downgrade steepened, and she pressed her brakes on the curve.

The car slowed slightly before it lurched forward. Her head flew backward at the sudden momentum. The resistance on the brake pedal had completely disappeared. She shoved her foot hard on the brake three times. "Come on!"

Her grasp on the steering wheel tightened as she fought to stay within her lane and lost. Thankfully no one else was on the road. The needle on the speedometer rose to fifty. The speed limit on the curves was thirty-five. The bend straightened a bit, but the downgrade would continue for the next three miles.

In roughly two miles, the viewpoint would appear. The trees would disappear, but the rock wall and a ninety-degree turn would mean that if she couldn't slow the car down, she would likely get the best view of all before plunging to her death.

She stomped on the brake pedal over and over. Her stomach threatened to lose her lunch. "What do I do? What do I do?" Her mind raced, frantic to find a solution.

Raven whimpered in the backseat and stuck her nose over the console between the seats. "Oh, not now, dog, please," Alexis cried. "I'm trying to save our lives!" She needed to get her head on straight. "Lord, we need help!"

The parking brake line was separate from the other brakes. She gasped. Yes, that would stop them. She'd walk home after that, never to drive the bucket of bolts again. She shoved the car into Neutral.

The speedometer rose to sixty, matching the pace of her heart.

She yanked on the parking brake, but it flung upward without resistance. Useless. Her breathing grew erratic. It should've worked.

The likelihood of all the brakes going out at once was...

Her insides shook. At this rate, she'd hyperventilate. Her car had been the only one in the trail parking lot. Everyone in town knew she drove it.

This was no accident.

Another curve approached fast. Too fast. She could drive into the trees, but the only way that would slow her down was if she steered directly into a tree trunk. It'd have been a worthwhile option if the car weren't traveling over sixty miles per hour. Her 1982 beauty didn't come equipped with airbags, so the outcome of that scenario was certain death.

She abandoned the pedals on the floor and placed her feet on either side to use as leverage while she took the second curve. She released a guttural cry as she did so.

*Please let Nick see what's going on, Lord.* She didn't know how he could possibly help, but she didn't think she could take even one hand off the steering wheel to reach for her cell phone.

The moment the road straightened, she looked in the rearview mirror and then ahead. Nothing in either direction but a sheer rock wall, trees and an upcoming deadly curve.

# FOUR

Nick cringed at the sound of branches hitting the side of his truck. He'd jogged through this area of the forest before so he could sit at his favorite bench overlooking the farmlands in the valley, but driving through the forest was another matter. He swerved and barely missed a thin aspen that seemed to come out of nowhere.

It was hard enough to motor through the foliage without the additional challenge of doing it at high speeds, downhill, as the sun dipped below the horizon. The perspiration dripped down his neck as he second-guessed the possibility his plan would work.

The stakes were high, though. At first he'd laughed when he realized how fast Alexis was going. Maybe she was an adrenaline junkie out to prove that her bucket of bolts had plenty of life left in it. But when her car swerved wildly and barely made it past the last curve, he knew she had to be in trouble.

He could've tried to overtake her on the road, but he was so far behind it seemed unlikely. The curve would take her far to the right before bringing her back to the left, while the forest next to the road was on a separate sharp incline. It seemed like the only way to catch up to her.

Another tree seemingly jumped out of nowhere into his path. He missed it, but an outstretched branch made contact. A sickening crack of metal preceded the side mirror flying off into the distance. Something in his peripheral vision begged his attention. He couldn't afford to take the time to look, but if he was right, he'd caught up to Alexis. In an instant, the car was gone again which likely meant she'd had to take another curve.

He was running out of forest. The curve she was on would buy him some time, but if he didn't beat her to the drop-off, it would be too late. He stomped the pedal to the floor. His truck bounced over a fallen log. The terrain dipped. His torso lurched forward as he fought gravity to remain upright.

A crunch echoed through the forest. He didn't even want to think about the condition of his axles after this.

A strong beam of light illuminated the trees a mere hundred feet ahead. He veered to the right as far as he could manage. Fifty feet later, he spotted the edge of the road. He just needed enough space between the trees to sneak through.

The truck nose pitched, and his head bounced off the steering wheel. The ground was about to disappear. The throbbing in his head threatened to slow him down. He squinted through the pain and yanked the wheel to the right. Another screech of metal confirmed his fears: he'd lost the left side mirror as well.

He couldn't think about anything but keeping his speed high. He was running out of time to save her.

The truck bounced as he bounded over the rough rock bordering the road. Except the road ended in just a few feet. Nick slammed on his brakes. He fought back nausea as he stared at the open sky. If he'd waited thirty seconds more before turning onto the road, he'd have driven off the cliff. Some hero he would've been.

He turned his head in the direction she'd be coming. A flash of light reflecting off metal came from just past the rock wall. Alexis would fly around that curve any second and face the ninety-degree turn. He shoved the truck into Park and looked out the passenger window to see the baby-blue Honda barreling toward him at an unimaginable speed.

If she didn't make the sharp curve, the mass of his truck would slow her down for about ten—maybe fifteen—feet, if he chose to be optimistic. He pulled up the parking brake and braced for impact.

The Honda hugged the rock wall. She was trying her best to make the turn, but the laws of physics would work against her. His heart pumped fast against his rib cage. Instead of seeming like the wisest move to help her, he found himself in a one-sided game of chicken. He couldn't take the chance that the truck would succeed and keep him on solid ground.

He flung off his seat belt, hopped out and sprinted toward the front of the truck as he heard the screech of her tires skidding out of control. The shriek of metal against metal filled the valley.

He pressed off the balls of his feet, diving to get out of the way, and strained his arms forward while airborne. A searing pain ripped through his hip as the corner of her car's front bumper scraped past him. The force of it twisted his body so that he was facing the sky as his back hit the ground and he slid toward the cliff.

Dirt and gravel flew up around him, pressing through his clothes, poking every inch of his back. He reached his hands out blindly. His fingertips found a branch, and as he slid past, he tightened his grip until he came to a stop.

He panted, trying to catch his breath while ignoring the pain in every part of his body. His elbows had escaped unscathed thanks to his flailing arms. Alexis! Had it worked?

He propped himself up on his elbows as he watched the Honda come to a standstill. His truck had moved to the very edge of the cliff. Maybe he could've remained inside after all and avoided the massive amounts of pain currently begging for his attention.

The truck groaned, teetered, tipped…and fell.

An unearthly groan escaped his lips. Crunching metal and booms rivaling thunder echoed throughout the valley. His mouth went dry.

The Honda door flung open, and a cry reached his ears before he could utter one himself. She was safe… unlike his gorgeous truck, but she was more important. Obviously. His head fell backward, his body and emotional energy utterly spent.

Moisture and soft fur brushed against his cheek.

"Nick. Nick!"

He opened his eyes to find Raven kissing his cheek. "I'm alive." He held up a hand to reassure the dog, and the dog licked it instead. His brain told his body to move, to get up, but his sore backside didn't respond. "Are you okay?" he asked instead.

Alexis's tear-filled eyes met his gaze. She nodded.

"My brakes wouldn't work." Her voice shook and her shoulders began to follow suit. "And…and I thought you were still in the car."

"It was a truck." Calling it a car would insult its memory, but in the back of his mind, he knew now wasn't the time to argue the point. "Do you think it was because your car was old or…"

Alexis held out her hands and helped pull him up to standing. If not for the stinging sensation in his palms, he would've enjoyed how soft her hands felt. She looked into his eyes as he fought against the discomfort in his back and straightened.

"It wasn't an accident," she said. She let go of him and pulled her phone out. "I'm calling the police." She frowned at the screen and jumped up, straining her arm, most likely in an effort to find a signal. On her tiptoes, she held the phone to her ear.

Light from above hit his eyes, which didn't make sense as the sun was setting. He turned his gaze ever so slightly to the top of the ridge above them. For a brief second he thought for sure he'd seen a man watching them.

It seemed possible, in his state of mind, that his eyes were playing tricks on him. Maybe it'd just been a flash of reflection from her shiny sandals.

The sun continued its rapid descent, but the colors in the sky illuminated the tower of rock above him enough for him to see a shadowed form kneel. It was almost as if someone was holding a…

"Gun." His insides seized up. No more time to lick his wounds. In one motion, he curled into a crouched position. His spine and muscles objected to the fast movement, but he fought through it. "Alexis, take cover! Gunman!"

The sound of tires fast approaching from the direction of town barely registered before a truck pulled up in front of him. Alexis lunged toward Nick, staying low enough that she was also underneath the cover of the silver truck. The passenger window rolled down and the man leaned toward them from the driver's side. "Everything okay?"

"Stay down, Gerald. Nick said there was a gunman."

The man in a ball cap flinched and looked around.

"On top of the ridge." Nick pointed upward.

Gerald stuck his head out of the driver's window. His shoulders relaxed, and he huffed. "There's nothing but a lone tree and a bird circling up there. Eyes can play tricks on you when the sun is setting."

Nick had never met the man, but Alexis seemed to know him, so maybe he was credible. He straightened to look for himself. Sure enough, there was nothing but pink and orange streaks in the sky.

He wasn't crazy, though. He'd seen someone, and the silver truck had apparently scared the person off. Odd. If the gunman had been part of the drug ring, Nick would've thought that knocking off another witness would have been nothing to them.

"You guys look a little rough for wear. Everything okay?" Gerald gestured at Alexis.

She looked down at her stained shirt and skirt, and then glanced at Nick, uncertainty crossing her face. "It's fair to say we've had a bad evening."

Nick remained silent. If she knew the man in the truck and wasn't gushing about what had happened to him, perhaps he'd be wise not to say anything, either. But if the man drove off, there was a chance the gunman would return. They needed him to stay until the police arrived. If Nick had to, he'd talk to the man until he was blue in the face.

"We had a little accident," Alexis said.

That was the understatement of the year.

Gerald leaned forward, straining his neck to see over the cliff from the comfort of his vehicle. "You certainly did. It's a good thing your truck went down in the river instead of causing a fire. Otherwise you really wouldn't have a chance with the voters, Mr. Kendrick." He winked and chuckled. "Not that you have any chance against me in the first place."

Nick flinched as he connected the dots. He leaned forward to see the face underneath the ball cap. This man was his neighbor and opponent?

Alexis kept her eyes on the ridge above them. While Nick could have a motive to lie about drugs being stashed on Gerald's property, he'd had to run away from the gunmen the same as she did. Besides, someone had messed with her brakes. If it hadn't been for Nick, it would've worked. So she couldn't fathom what reason he'd have to lie about a gunman on the ridge. Whoever had been there would've had the perfect view if she'd wrecked.

She shivered involuntarily. What was taking the police so long? While she had no doubt that Gerald would hear about the incident on his land eventually, she didn't want to be the one who told him.

"Did this out-of-towner make you crash?" Gerald asked Alexis, a teasing lilt to his voice. Despite his smile, his eyes looked a little red, as if he'd either suffered an allergy attack or heard some upsetting news.

Nick's jaw tensed. "I think I've earned resident status if my name is on the ballot."

After the day she'd had, the last thing Alexis needed was to be the only audience member for an impromptu political debate. "Nick saved my life. My brakes stopped working."

Gerald shook his head. "I know you don't want to hear this, but take it from me. There's a point when it's time to put a car to rest, Alexis. I make more money keeping cars in business, so you know I'm not lying."

She didn't need a lecture. Her car's age hadn't been the problem. If Gerald had anything to do with the men on his property, then it followed that he would want her dead, as well.

Her parents had considered him their trusted mechanic for most of her life, so she wanted to think Chief Spencer had the right idea. The more likely scenario was that Gerald had been used as a pawn. She'd learned time and time again, though, that she wasn't the best judge of character.

She smiled and nodded as Gerald finished his speech on when a car wasn't worth repairing.

"Gerald, I promise I'll look for another vehicle soon. Word on the streets was you were out of town for the holiday weekend, visiting family."

Nick flashed her a knowing look. Judging by his posture, he didn't want to confront Gerald about the incident, either. Probably wise, as they were on a cliff without a vehicle or a place to hide.

Gerald shrugged. "You know how family can be.

Visit got cut short." He looked forward at the road. "Do you need me to call you a tow truck?"

Raven nuzzled her nose against Nick.

Gerald paled. "Whose dog is that?"

"I'm pet-sitting," Alexis answered. "Client confidentiality." There probably wasn't such a thing in the pet-sitting business, but it rolled off her tongue so fast that she was shocked at how the words stung.

She hated the memory of those words as they'd been barked at her during the disbarment hearing. Thankfully no one in town, aside from her parents, knew of her shame, and she wanted to keep it that way. It'd made her nervous to find out that Nick had come from Seattle.

Her story had made *The Seattle Times*, but as far as she knew, her photograph hadn't been released. Alexis Thompson wasn't a rare name, so she hoped no one would ever find out.

A siren sounded once behind the truck. Gerald flinched and waved into the rearview mirror. "Looks like they'll take care of you. Have a safe weekend, Lexi."

Jeremy stepped out of the cruiser. "Now, didn't I just tell you that thing was an accident waiting to happen?" He flung his arm in the direction of the blue car. "You could have died!" He frowned at the sight of Nick's scraped up arms and ripped clothes. "What happened to you? I'll call for an ambulance."

Nick waved away his concern. "I'm beat up, but there's no need for emergency care." He pointed upward. "There was someone watching us from up there. Possibly a gunman. Can you send someone to check it out?"

Alexis stepped forward, not waiting for Jeremy to answer. "This wasn't my fault. The car was perfectly fine earlier. But when I picked it up from the parking lot, the brakes felt mushy, and then suddenly they went out."

Jeremy looked back and forth between the two of them. "That doesn't mean—"

"And the parking brake was out, too." She hadn't meant to shout. She pulled her shoulders back. She couldn't handle it if one more person implied it was because of her poor judgment in driving a junker that this had happened. Yes, she drove an old car. Yes, it was hilarious for a lawyer to own a junker. It wasn't relevant. Someone had sabotaged her car.

Jeremy closed his mouth. He turned his gaze upward. "I don't see anyone now. And there's no one to send. I'm it. All our officers are on calls or on vacation. I've been told this is usually a quiet weekend for us."

He turned, and his eyebrows rose as he stared out into the valley, his focus on Nick's truck. "I'll admit, the parking brake not working makes it a little more suspicious. Everyone knows your car..." He let his words trail off as his brow furrowed. "It was sitting in the parking lot at the trailhead for quite a while after your interaction with suspected drug runners. That's if Nick was right about what he saw." He seemed to be talking to himself more than them.

She tilted her head. "Mine was the only vehicle at the trailhead, Jeremy. It wouldn't be hard to figure out I owned it."

Jeremy sucked in a breath through his nostrils and exhaled loudly. "I'll take your theory to the chief, but we're going to have to do an official investigation before I can confirm it's foul play, Alexis. If you're right, it should be obvious that someone tampered with the lines."

She placed her hands on her hips. "Okay. What now?"

"I'll see what Chief wants to do, but I can give you both a ride home, where you can wait to hear from us. I've already got a call in to a tow truck for your car."

It didn't seem wise to leave Nick at his house without a vehicle, especially since the gunmen probably knew that was where he lived now. "Take us both to my house."

Nick turned his head, his eyebrows high.

"I have an extra car." Alexis sighed. "It's my dad's. You can drive it until we get everything sorted out." She saw the objection in his expression. "I'm in town. Everywhere I need to go is in walking distance. You can use the car to go back and forth from your place to your practice until we take care of insurance. I insist. Besides, the rental place is already closed for the day. It's the least I can do for getting you in this mess. You saved my life." Her throat closed as the last few hours overwhelmed her. "Twice," she whispered.

"Okay, then. That's settled." Jeremy looked Nick up and down and pointed to his scrapes. "You sure you don't need medical treatment? You're not going to self-treat, are you, Doc?"

"Besides some bandages and ointment? No. I don't prescribe myself any pain medicine."

She gave the leash a tug to lead Raven to the squad car. "Vets can write themselves prescriptions?"

He shrugged. "It happens, but I think it's a potential

gateway to drug abuse that I'm not willing to tempt. If I need anything, I'll go to Urgent Care."

He certainly seemed to know a lot about the illegal drug trade.

Jeremy opened the back door to the squad car. Alexis groaned. They would have to drive into town on the main drag. She didn't mind riding in a police cruiser when they were out on the edges of town where no one would see them, but if Jeremy drove into town with her in the backseat, the rumor mill would go into full effect.

Her parents would hear about it clear in Arizona by morning. They didn't need to add to their worries about her. "Um, maybe I could ride in the front?"

Nick swung his gaze to her so fast she worried about his neck. His look said it all. He wished he'd called shotgun first. She almost gloated until she remembered that his truck was at the bottom of the valley because of her. He sported injuries because of her. And, since he was running for town mayor, she could grudgingly admit he had more at stake if his reputation was ruined.

Jeremy shrugged. "Sure. It's open."

"You take the front," Alexis told Nick. "I'll—" she swallowed "—sit with the dog."

"You don't like dogs."

"We have the entire backseat. She can keep her distance."

Nick eyed her for a minute. Indecision played across his features. He seemed the type always to put a lady's needs first. Seemed? No, judging by his actions today, he was.

"I'm sure, Nick."

Jeremy put his fists on his waist. "I don't care who goes where, but if you don't decide, I'm going to drive off without either of you."

She slid into the backseat before Nick could argue. Raven followed without hesitation and tried to rest her head on Alexis's knee, but Alexis shooed her away.

Maybe she could lean her head down so her hair would cover most of her face when they entered town. Of course, that kind of posture would make her look guilty of something. She could lean back and bravely smile. Or would that make her look crazy and high on something?

Jeremy started the cruiser, and a sudden illogical need to get out of the car gripped her. No one could've messed with his brakes, though. She inhaled as the car took the sharp turn. Normally she enjoyed the curvy drive from the trail down to town as if it was a mild roller coaster that she controlled, but it was too soon after her brush with death to be in a car again.

Her right hand clung to the door's armrest. How often did they clean and sanitize the inside of police cruisers? She cringed and let go. A hot shower had never sounded so good.

The dog slid along the vinyl seat until its backside hit the opposite side of the car. Raven jumped up on all fours, seemingly alarmed as they approached another curve.

"Sit. Lie down." Alexis patted the spot next to her.

The dog obeyed. Alexis tensed as she allowed Raven's head to rest on her lap. She placed her other arm on top of the dog's torso to make sure it didn't slide around anymore. Oh, Theresa would be hearing about every single detail of this afternoon and evening over many dinners. Or chocolate bars. Or both.

The warmth from the dog slowed her own heart rate slightly. She looked down to see Raven gazing up at her. It was hard not to smile in response. She cleared her throat and stared ahead.

Jeremy glanced at Nick. "I hope you have good insurance. I don't envy you trying to get money out of a lawyer." He winked at Alexis in the rearview mirror.

Alexis fought the instinct to roll her eyes, but the dread at having to swap insurance information and the interrogation the claim adjusters would run her through made her limbs heavy. "What are we going to do to make sure something like this doesn't happen anymore? How do we know they won't target us again? Jeremy, what are you guys going to do about it?"

Jeremy shook his head. "I can't comment on that, Alexis. It's on the chief's radar, and we'll be investigating. It's a high priority."

Nick huffed. "I think it's in our best interest to be proactive."

"Well, Alexis knows everyone in town. If she didn't know—"

"Not everyone," she objected. "I'd never met Nick, and I certainly didn't recognize the guy—the scout—who took a pic of us. I didn't see the faces of any of the men who had guns, but I would've thought their outlines, their backs, would've sparked some guess as to who they were. I've got nothing. So, not likely."

Nick sagged against his headrest. "Ever dealt with something like this before?"

Jeremy shook his head. "No. We don't have too many drug problems here."

"You are right off the interstate—The Corridor. It may not be openly a problem, but I guarantee it is. There's not a town, city or county that hasn't been touched, and ignorance is the greatest risk to this town."

His impassioned voice stirred her. He wasn't just a walking dictionary on the drug problem in their region. This seemed personal. Her curiosity almost got the better of her, but she fought it off. She'd asked enough of the man for one night.

Jeremy stiffened. "I'm not ignorant."

She could've cut the tension in the air with a knife.

"I didn't mean you personally," Nick said. "I apologize if it sounded that way."

Jeremy didn't respond, and they rode in silence. Stars began to twinkle in the sky. A few minutes later the decline and curves flattened out. They were about to enter town.

Alexis exhaled. She could move the dog away now but something kept her from doing so. The warmth wasn't unpleasant. She certainly wasn't a dog person yet, and probably never would be, but as long as Raven didn't start drooling on her skirt, she supposed the dog could stay put. Alexis straightened and pulled her hand back. She didn't need to hold the dog's torso anymore.

She let her hand rest on top of Raven's neck, just below the makeshift collar Nick had rigged from the leash. Something hot, wet and sticky met her skin.

Alexis yanked her hand back.

Blood.

# FIVE

Nick kneeled in the driveway where Officer Jeremy had dropped them off. He pushed back Raven's fur to see the matted area of blood. The dim lighting didn't help him reach a confident diagnosis. "I can't be sure, but it might need stitches. If she breaks into a run anytime soon, it could gape open."

"How do you think it happened?" Her face looked pinched.

"There wasn't any glass in your car," he mused. Raven stayed still while he took a second look at the jagged cut. "The barbed wire fence had to be the culprit."

"But I lifted her over it. You took her from me."

"The second time, yes. The first time, she zipped underneath it in hot pursuit of that squirrel." Raven's ears perked at the last word, and she looked around hopefully.

"Oh." She worried her hands together. "I didn't know. She didn't whimper."

"Dogs don't openly express pain every time. And adrenaline might have played a part." He straightened to standing. "I'd like to take her to my office and examine her."

Alexis nodded rapidly. "Whatever you think is best."

She looked slightly pale, come to think of it.

"Are you okay?" He reached a steadying hand toward her arm. The softness of her skin jolted him, but she didn't seem too hot or too cold. He wasn't a physician, but he had spent a short amount of time in medical school before deciding it wasn't the right field for him. "Can you tell me how you're feeling? Do you have a problem with blood?"

"I'm fine." She shook her head. "I mean, I don't know. I feel horrible that she got hurt on my watch. It's my fault. I've done everything wrong. Theresa never should've entrusted me with the dog."

In his opinion, the blame rested with Theresa for asking so much of her friend. "There's no need to feel guilty. If you've never been a pet owner, there's no reason to think you'd know about breakaway collars."

Alexis sucked in a gasp. "I haven't reached Theresa. I need to let her know what's happened. That the dog is hurt." She pointed at Raven, but her eyes drifted to the dried blood on her hand, and her face lost what little color it had left.

"How about you wash up first?"

She nodded. "Okay." She turned to the house. "I'll get you the keys to my dad's sedan. I can join you at your office in a few minutes."

He hadn't argued with her earlier, but Nick would not leave a single woman alone without a vehicle all night when there was potential she was still in danger. Officer Jeremy had promised Alexis that an officer would make regular rounds past her house all night, but there was no mention of what "regular rounds" entailed. If they were short on officers, who knew how often someone would actually check up on her?

Nick was accustomed to making fast decisions. He had the impression that Alexis tended to do so, as well. So he'd argue over the car issue later, after he took care of Raven. Besides, he'd likely need complete focus when arguing with a lawyer.

"I'll walk. It's just across the street. See you in a few." He bent down and ignored the pinch in his back as he lifted Raven into his arms. For now, he wanted Raven immobile so the bleeding would continue to diminish.

"Um, okay."

He walked across the street. Not a block away, he punched in the pass code and unlocked the employee side door. The undeniable smell of animals combined with soft meows, chirps and barks greeted him. Raven shifted and shivered in his arms. "It's okay, girl. It's normal to be nervous, but there's no need."

He set her down to hang out alone in an exam room with a treat while he turned on lights, unlocked the front door for Alexis and gathered his supplies. Raven was so enamored with the brushing chew that Nick could trim the fur and clean the area around the wound without assistance. "That's going to help your breath, too, girl. Might help Alexis like you," he said in soothing tones.

"I've never heard of good dog breath winning a girl over." Alexis stood in the doorway. She'd replaced her skirt, blouse and sandals with jeans, a gray T-shirt and canvas shoes. Her hair was pulled back into a loose ponytail.

Nick's stomach heated. "Talking to animals while I work helps soothe them."

Alexis stepped closer. Raven wagged her tail at the sight. "I couldn't reach Theresa."

"Well, you tried." He pointed to the bench. "Please sit there and hold the leash for me." He lifted the prepared syringe and pulled up the loose skin above the wound to inject a painkiller. "It would help if you kept her head in your lap. I need her calm and still." He turned to prep the needle for sutures. She frowned with concern. "Don't worry. I'm fast," he added.

She bit her lower lip and nodded.

"If you stroke her head and talk to her, she won't feel anything but a bit of tugging." He told himself he wasn't trying to win her over to dogs. Keeping the dog motionless was in its best interest.

"I'm not talking to an animal." She bent her head and rested her hand on top of Raven. Raven pulled her ears back and looked up at Alexis in response.

She sighed. "How about I talk to you instead while I look at her?" Her voice took on a soothing quality.

The research on what dogs could understand was conflicted. Some estimated a Labrador could obtain the same level of vocabulary as a toddler, but other research pointed to the tone of voice as the method for understanding. "I'll take what I can get." He needed to keep her talking while he worked, then. Fortunately, he had a ton of questions about her. "Tell me what kind of law you used to practice." In his peripheral vision he could see her stiffen.

"Patent law."

Well, so far he wasn't getting her to talk much. Nick prepared the needle for sutures. "Was that your passion? Patent law?"

She laughed. "Uh, no. It made for a well-paying first job, though. My real hope was to get my feet wet, get some money saved up and then transition to elder law. There aren't enough people advocating for senior citizens."

He loved the lilt in her voice while she talked at the dog. A former lawyer who wanted to fight for the rights of senior citizens would be perfect to lead his team of volunteers. The cops seemed to think she knew most everyone in town. The combination could be the answer to his prayers about the campaign.

"So why didn't you?" he asked. They sounded ridiculous talking to each other in higher-pitched, soft voices, but Raven remained calm. Nick had three stitches done. Just a couple more and he would tie it off. Thankfully, there was no way Raven would be able to lick or chew on this part of her back. It should heal nicely.

Her eyes flicked upward before landing back on Raven. "Life happens. Plans change."

There was pain behind her eyes. He knew she was here to help her parents, but she said they weren't ill and had moved to Arizona. The chief and Officer Jeremy both seemed to respect her, so she couldn't have done something seedy. Maybe she'd stopped practicing law because a loved one had died, or she'd suffered a bad breakup with a coworker.

If any of those were the case, needing time to heal before going back into such a stressful career made sense. He certainly wouldn't be able to handle being a lawyer. "So you'll be here until you sell your parents' house?"

"Yes. That's the plan for now."

A lawyer who enjoyed her job would've outsourced the task to a real-estate agent and contractors, wouldn't she? So that couldn't be the real reason she was still in town. But it was yet another reminder that she had no interest in putting down roots in Barings.

"Houses don't seem to be selling very fast here," he finally said. He swirled the thread into a final knot. "It's something I hope to change if we can bring some new business into town. I imagine temp work isn't exactly challenging for someone with your experience. It's usually entry-level work. Am I right?"

She no longer looked at the dog but stared right at him. "I can see you have an excellent bedside manner, Nick. But I feel like you're trying to lead up to telling me something. Since this isn't my dog and she doesn't need some drastic treatment, give it to me straight. What are you getting at?" She raised her eyebrows. "I can tell you right now I won't be willing to temp as your vet tech or even as a receptionist." She scrunched her nose. "I couldn't handle being around dogs all day even if you doubled my pay."

He grinned. Yes. She was a straight shooter, which was exactly what he needed. "You're right, but I don't need another tech or receptionist. I've been running my mayoral campaign all by myself. I've got only a couple of months before the vote, and I've been praying to find someone who knows everyone in this town, who understands laws and policies. I thought it was a tall-order prayer, but here you are. I'm not flush with cash, but I imagine I can pay you as much as a temp job could in this town. Would you consider being my campaign manager?"

Her jaw dropped and eyes widened. "No. Absolutely not."

"Because you're voting for Gerald?"

She flinched. "Gerald? No."

"Is it the money? We haven't even talked numbers yet. I could settle for part-time and you wouldn't leave anyone in the lurch. What's her name—Theresa? I'm sure we could work something out."

She scrunched up her forehead. "It's not that." Raven seemed to realize he was done working on her and flopped down to the floor.

He raised his eyebrows. "Is it because I said I prayed? That I'm a Christian?"

She stood. "No." She walked toward the door, turned around to face him, opened her mouth and promptly shut it again. She looked like she was in a daze as she crossed the lobby and rested her hands on the door.

His heart raced as Raven stood by his side, watching Alexis leave with him. He'd known she might turn him down, but her reaction—almost as if he was too vile to consider—threw him for a loop. She could've at least let him down easy. He really was fun to work with, at least according to his employees.

Her shoulders sagged as she looked out into the street. "It's not you, Nick. It's nothing about you. I can see you are a good man, and you might even be what this town needs, for all I know. I just can't help you." She swallowed but still didn't make eye contact. "Thank you for asking."

She looked tired and wounded. He wanted to ask, to help, but it seemed clear he'd never be able to breach the invisible barrier surrounding her. In the end, it wasn't any of his business, though the mystery would drive him crazy. "Fair enough," he finally said. "End of discussion."

She nodded, relief evident as she sighed. "I forgot to bring the car keys with me."

"I'm not taking the car. I'm staying here tonight."

Her wide eyes swung to meet his. "Why?"

Several reasons came to mind. The practice had a good alarm system and would elicit a faster police response time than if he went home. The men knew where he lived, which probably meant it wasn't safe. The most important reason to him, though, was that she wouldn't have a reason to insist he take the car and she wouldn't be left without transportation, but he felt sure she'd object if he voiced it aloud. "I have a cot and a change of clothes here. And this way, my receptionist can give me a ride out to the car rental office in the morning."

She studied him for a moment. "Okay. Then I'm feeding you dinner. Come over as soon as you can."

It wasn't a question, and for a split second, he almost refused on reflex. People weren't in the habit of telling him what to do, and as a strong-willed man, he wasn't in the habit of taking orders...at least without being asked nicely. His stomach, however, rumbled at the thought of dinner, and it was nice of her to think of it. After the day they'd had, they both probably needed extra grace in how they addressed each other. "Okay. If I leave now, it'll give Keri—the teen who comes to take care of the animals during boarding—a chance to feed and play with them without feeling like she's being watched."

Suspecting that a photo of Alexis and him was out there, circling among drug runners, Nick wished he could say the same.

Alexis moved to open the front door. Why did she need a conscience? Most of her life would likely have been easier without one complicating matters. Being a lawyer certainly would've been easier.

Nick's supposed reason that he wanted to sleep in the veterinary hospital sounded weak to her. She could see right through him. He was doing it to make sure she had a car. He'd already saved her life…twice. As if that wasn't enough heroism for the day.

So, since saying thank you seemed like the understatement of the year, the least she could do was make sure he had more dinner options than wet or dry dog food. But in reality, the last thing she wanted was to spend more time with Nick.

"Wait up. It's dark out," Nick said. "Let me put Raven in a kennel with some food and water, and I'll walk you out."

She bristled. There he went again, making sure she'd stay safe. She wasn't going to argue, though, because he had a point, but she hated owing him so much. How could she repay a debt to him that kept growing? It had almost killed her to say no when he'd asked for help with the campaign, but she also wasn't ready to tell him why her help would effectively ruin his chances at the position.

"I'm going to try Theresa again," she said. She could hear the edge in her own voice. The Lord might have kept her conscience in good working condition, but He hadn't curbed her pride yet. Not that she was asking Him to help work on that. No, thank you. She'd already suffered enough humiliation to last a lifetime. Unfortunately, instead of humility, she felt more insecure while simultaneously defensive.

"Thanks for offering to walk me," she called out after Nick and Raven. She looked through the glass door at the stars, hoping the Lord could see she had acknowledged and, at least outwardly, amended her prideful attitude. It would be great if the Lord could round up the drug runners who wanted her dead while He was at it.

A silver station wagon drove down the road. Alexis pulled back from the glass door. The lone streetlight at the corner had never bothered her before, but she'd never felt in danger on her own street before, either.

The dogs in the back of Nick's practice sounded happy to see him, assuming barking could sound happy. If Theresa answered the call, she'd be shocked at the background noise. Alexis held the phone up to her ear as it started to ring. Three rings, four…and it connected to voice mail. Alexis didn't want to leave a message. She opted to text:

Need you to call. Urgent. Bad things happened today. You need to come back home.

Alexis studied her own message before she pressed Send. While she didn't begrudge Theresa a chance at fun and time with her mysterious boyfriend, she really needed to take over the care and decisions for Raven. Once again, Alexis's mind drifted to who the potential boyfriend could be. If Theresa had known him all her life, maybe it was the owner of Barings Heating and Air. When Alexis had temped as a receptionist for the guy, he'd been very eager to know how Theresa was doing. And he was a recent widower, which would cause tongues to wag around town that it was too soon for the man to date. So that would explain the secrecy. Alexis grinned at the thought. They would make a good couple. Theresa deserved a kind, thoughtful man in her life.

"Good news?" Nick asked. "Something must've made you smile."

She tried not to react at his appearance. He'd not only put Raven away but also taken the time to change into a light blue dress shirt and brown dress pants complete with a belt. Alexis knew that the clothes did not make the man, but they certainly didn't hurt. He must have kept extra clothes at the office. Smart, given his occupation.

"No news," she said. "Daydreaming about happier things."

He raised an eyebrow and placed a hand on his stomach. "Dinner, perhaps?"

A nervous laugh escaped, and Alexis realized with horror that she'd been twirling the end of her ponytail. While it was just an unconscious habit whenever she got flustered, she knew it looked flirtatious—her girlfriends had teased her about it mercilessly in college.

She dropped her hand to her side. "I'm afraid dinner is not likely to be dream-worthy." She pushed open the door, and he followed her to the street. "I'm still using up my mom's freezer meals and emptying her pantry. She has enough to last until Thanksgiving."

"I'm sure it'll be wonderful." His stomach growled as if in answer. "Raven is enjoying her food. Keri will be in there soon to give her more attention, as well."

They crossed the street to the driveway. In the distance, toward the end of the block, the silver car she'd seen pass earlier sat on the side of the road. She squinted. "Does it look like someone is in that car?"

"I can't tell." His eyes widened in the moonlight. "Should I be concerned?"

Across from the car were two houses, both rentals. She didn't know who'd moved into those particular ones since she'd been back, which proved that she didn't know every single person in the town, despite Jeremy's assumptions. "I think the events of the day have made me paranoid," she finally said.

Her statement wasn't entirely truthful. She'd been paranoid for months, ever since hearing a confession from a murderer, from someone she'd thought was a nice man.

Nick kept his gaze on the car. "Paranoid or not, caution should be the order of the day. Let's get inside and let your cop friend know. Silver Subaru Outback." He shook his head. "That model's popularity is basically tied with the pickup truck in Idaho."

"It makes sense. Everyone wants all-wheel drive around here. I imagine it'll be my next vehicle."

Her parents' living room's bay window faced the driveway and the street. She rounded the corner and pulled the keys out of her jeans to unlock the brown entry door, which faced the garage, making a corridor of sorts between the two unattached buildings.

Two pots of wilting geraniums sat on either side of

the front door. She'd been so busy she hadn't noticed until now. She glanced up at Nick, hoping he didn't notice, but he still had his eyes on the street. If any prospective buyers actually came to look at the house, dying flowers probably wouldn't help win them over.

Nick crossed the threshold right behind her and closed the door. He slipped off his shoes before following her onto the plush beige carpet. The house took on a new appearance before her eyes as she saw it in a new light, imagining she hadn't spent a lifetime in it.

The bookshelves and walls were covered in framed photographs. Her mother had never been fond of knickknacks or artwork but loved to be surrounded by images of the people she loved. Fake potted flowers were in almost every corner of the living room, in addition to the two recliners and love seat. Maybe she could switch out the dying flowers for some of the fake ones. The spot where the television had resided was empty. The relatively new flat screen had taken the trip to Arizona with them.

Nick ignored it all, crossed the room and placed a knee on her favorite spot in the entire house, the cushioned ledge of the bay window. He leaned forward and peeked out the sheer curtains. "Car is still there, but I don't see anyone in the driver's seat."

"Then it's probably nothing. It is Labor Day weekend. Families like to come visit." Or so she'd been told. She didn't have many extended relatives closer than Texas, and she'd never visited there.

Nick's face looked pinched. Either he was really hungry or something she'd said had sparked pain.

"I have Jeremy's number, though. I'll let him know,

to be safe." She sent him a quick text. The phone vibrated in response. "He says someone will drive by soon." Knowing an officer would check out the car, she felt the tension in her back loosen a little.

She hustled to preheat the oven before she grabbed a bag of premade burritos out of the freezer. Sweet potato fries didn't really complement the dish, but they were the only vegetable she could find.

Nick put his hands behind his back and perused the photographs on the shelves. "Wait a second." He turned to look at her, his finger pointing at the photo of her father receiving an award for public service from the governor. "Was your dad the mayor at one point?"

She dumped all of the food onto a cookie sheet and shoved it into the oven, not bothering to wait for it to preheat. She'd never claimed to be a good cook. She got too impatient. "Yes. He served for most of my childhood and adulthood, until Gerald took his spot last term."

Nick's pensive nod said it all. He was making the assumption that her dad's political history was the reason she'd said no to his campaign manager job. There was a grain of truth to it. Her dad had hoped to move on from being a mayor to campaigning for senator. He'd held off during her rebellious teen years but thought maybe enough time had passed for him to run. When her little "hiccup," as her dad called her disbarment, happened, he decided maybe it would be best to retire early, for her sake.

Heat flooded her chest. She wished she'd never opened up to Nick. He made it way too easy, though, as he had such a kind face and demeanor. His silent smile practically begged her to say more. It's why she'd admitted to him that her passion was elder law when she could count on one hand how many people she'd told.

She knew what he was thinking, what the whole town was probably thinking. It didn't make sense for a lawyer to take so long prepping a house for sale. She could've flown out for a weekend or hired people to do it. Good lawyers had money. They had luxury vehicles. They weren't wasting their skills working entry-level jobs at a temp agency.

If she was honest with herself, she still wanted to go into elder law, but she hadn't gotten up enough nerve to plead her case to the Idaho State Bar. Her license was revoked in Washington, but there was a slim-to-none chance she could be allowed to serve in her home state.

Once she built up enough courage to do that, her past would no longer be a secret. The entire town would hear about it. She'd have to travel to Boise to appear before the Bar. Boise wasn't too far away, and plenty of people from Barings had relatives there. Someone would find out, she just knew it. And if she lost, her last hope of moving on would be dashed. She wasn't ready to face it. Not yet.

Nick stepped into the kitchen and nodded at the office nook nestled between the counter and the dining table. "Would it be okay to borrow a piece of paper and pencil?"

"Of course. Dinner won't be long now."

"Proverbs 31." He pointed at the Bible she'd left open on the counter. "Good stuff."

She blushed. Had it really been just this morning she'd been rereading that? "Most people think of the wife of noble character." She tried to ignore the approving look in his eyes. "But there are two verses in there that I clung to as a lawyer, which, come to think of it, you might appreciate. My dad pointed them out to me many years ago."

His eyebrows rose. "Oh?"

"Verses 8 and 9 basically say we should speak up for those who don't have a voice, for those who need defending, for justice…" She let her voice trail off when she realized how passionate she sounded. Her neck heated again. She grabbed some glasses and filled them with iced tea.

"I appreciate you sharing that with me," he said, his voice soft. "Is that why you wanted to practice elder law?"

"Partly." She'd gone and gotten personal again. She focused on the food. The house was devoid of every other Labor Day weekend staple. Her menu was as weird as her life lately.

Nick had taken a spot at the dining table and appeared to be sketching something. Maybe he was one of those people who liked to color to relax. Personally, she couldn't understand the compulsion. The only thing that could relax her was jotting down every single thing on her mind, like an epic to-do list, and then following it up with an engrossing book to forget it all until she could start crossing things off. Maybe that's why she made a good lawyer. *Had* made a good lawyer.

She peeked over his shoulder. Rough short lines

formed a misshapen circle. "Are you drawing a turtle?" Did he treat turtles? "One of your patients?"

He twisted his torso to look at her, an amused smile on his face. She smiled in response, not even knowing why and fighting the urge to twirl her hair again. "No," he said slowly. "I was trying to be proactive and draw the scout's face as best as I could remember. I know I'm not the best artist in the wor—"

"Clearly." She laughed at his facial expression and held up both hands. "Sorry. I'm no artist, either, but it's not a bad idea. We both saw him." She pulled out the chair beside him and took a seat.

"Exactly. If we could agree on what he looked like, then maybe the authorities would have a better shot at getting him."

"Yes, but how much good would that do us? He still sent our picture out to the drug network or whatever they call themselves."

"We don't know he did that for sure, but even if that's the case, at least we've started somewhere." He tapped the sketch. "Maybe the authorities could get this guy to talk. At the very least, it should help in getting the runners to back off. Awareness is our greatest weapon. The more people who know what we're dealing with here, the better."

An annoying repetitive noise interrupted her next thought. It sounded like a faraway car alarm. She stood and crossed to the bay window. "The Outback is gone." She shifted her view to the right. A flicker of light from what looked like the back of his practice made her pause.

A dark figure could be seen running toward the

building. The orange light grew. "Nick—" Her throat closed. The animals…

Nick rushed forward and put a hand on her back as he peered forward. "What is it?"

Her hands shook as she pulled out her phone. "Fire."

# SIX

Nick barely had the presence of mind to shove on his shoes before sprinting across the street. He passed Alexis, but his legs and arms felt weighted. He couldn't run as fast as he wanted. The shrill pitch of the fire alarm grew louder as he got closer. Flames licked the back of the building and could be seen on the roof.

"Keri," he screamed, scanning the sides of the property. The sixteen-year-old girl should've been tending to the boarded animals by now. What if she was trapped inside with them? He couldn't imagine the sprinkler system he'd installed in the boarding area would be a match against the vicious blaze for very long. The smoke alone...

"They're coming," Alexis yelled, mere steps behind him. She panted. "Fire trucks are coming."

He didn't bother to reply. Emergency personnel should've already been on the way if the alarm system was working properly. He attempted to slow down, but his knee hit the front door as he tried to pull it open. Locked. He keyed in the code to unlock it. The second it took for the little light to turn green seemed like an eternity.

He swung the door open. The smoke dimmed the lights in the lobby, and the acrid smell almost bowled him over. The deafening beeping of the alarm was accompanied by at least one howling dog. "Stay back." He waved Alexis away as he charged forward and hunkered down.

The strobes from the firelights illuminated the door he wanted. He yanked it open and Keri, drenched from the sprinklers and holding a carrier, almost barreled into him. She screamed. Then her eyes widened. "Oh, Dr. Kendrick." She burst into tears. "The back door. Someone blocked it. Most of the dogs are out—" Keri launched into a fit of coughing.

"Go!" They could figure out what had happened after everyone was safe. He stepped aside. Alexis had ignored his plea to stay out of the way. She grabbed the cat carrier from Keri and ran her toward the front door.

Nick put his arm over his mouth and tried to squint through the smoke. The left wall had flames licking it, but the sprinkler system on that side was squirting out a steady stream. Not enough to put the fire completely out, but to keep it from spreading.

He followed the howling until he reached the kennel. Raven sat shivering and shaking, wet and clearly scared. His heart twisted as he unlatched the kennel and picked up the dog. The second half of the sprinklers sprayed down on them. The blaze licked the surrounding walls now. He needed to make sure there were no more animals in danger.

Alexis appeared at his side. He startled. He didn't risk opening his mouth, but he wanted to scream at her to get out. She threw her arms around Raven, pulled her from him and darted out the door.

Nick ran throughout the small area, flinging doors open. Daisy, the golden retriever with a wounded paw, remained. Otherwise the boarding area was empty. He lifted the seventy-pound, full-grown animal and struggled to keep her still as he ran with her into the lobby.

Alexis and Raven cowered against the side wall. A ceiling beam had fallen, flames devouring it. They were trapped.

Nick stepped up onto the receptionist's office chair, stood on the desk and fumbled to open the window with one arm. He shoved the pane upward and felt before he heard the whoosh of flames coming his way.

He jumped off the desk with Daisy in his arms. The flames on the ceiling hungrily headed for the side window. Alexis touched the handle to the exam room door hesitantly before she opened it. It was smart thinking. There was a large front window in there, but as it was for decorative purposes, there was no way to open it. He grabbed the large glass jar of treats sitting next to the exam station and waved Alexis back. He pitched the jar at the center of the window. The glass cracked, then shattered into a million little pieces.

Alexis didn't wait for his instructions. She stepped onto the bench she'd sat on a mere hour ago and launched forward, with Raven in her arms, out the ground floor window. Nick joined her a second later with the wriggling Daisy. He gulped the air greedily, too greedily, as he began coughing.

Flashing lights sped down the street and pulled into his empty parking lot. The volunteer firefighters poured out of the red truck and set to work as EMTs rushed at him and pulled him to safety.

Daisy began shaking in his arms. "She needs oxygen."

"Sir, I need to take care of you first."

"Give her oxygen," Nick repeated. He spun frantically until he spotted Alexis and Keri being treated by another EMT. "If they're okay, give the black dog and the cat oxygen, too."

"Sir…"

Nick saw the uncertainty in the young man's eyes. He knew some states had passed laws allowing emergency personnel to treat animals, but he wasn't sure if Idaho was one of them. If it turned out to be a liability issue, he'd take responsibility. "I'm a veterinarian. Let me."

The EMT didn't say a word as Nick gently set Daisy down. The flames overtaking his practice barely registered until the dog stopped shivering. He pointed at a policeman. "You. Come watch this dog for me."

The policeman frowned but didn't argue, compassion in his eyes as the dog's front paw bandages registered. Nick hustled over to Raven and administered the oxygen. Alexis met his eyes, soot covering her cheeks and nose. "You were brilliant," he said. He turned to Keri. "I can't thank you enough. The other dogs we were boarding weren't in there. Are all the other dogs in the pen?"

She nodded, tears still streaming down her cheeks. "I had taken them out for playtime before bed. But when I looked back, I saw flames. I ran inside—" she coughed for a minute "—but after I grabbed the kitty," she sobbed, "the back door wouldn't open."

The chief stood behind her. He had heard the whole thing. His face turned a purplish hue as he took a knee and pulled her into a hug. "You were a hero, Keri. A hero."

Tears filled Nick's eyes. Alexis sniffed beside him. "Keri is Chief Spencer's niece."

The chief's hard eyes met Nick's. "I will make sure to take down whoever is responsible." His chilled voice seemed to be implying it was Nick's fault somehow. He wouldn't even dignify the threat with a response.

The cat was the hardest to treat. Nick's arms took the brunt of the scratches as he tried to make sure the cat wasn't suffering from smoke inhalation.

Alexis wiped the tears from under her eyes. "What do you need me to do, Doc?"

He didn't know where to begin. The practice… the… He took a deep breath. The animals came first, and he needed more hands. He passed her his phone. "Could you call my staff? Abigail and Marla? They're in my contacts. Ask them to get in touch with any owners who are still in town, then get down here and help me find places for these animals tonight."

Her eyes widened. "On it."

Nick went on autopilot. Alexis wordlessly followed him as he guided Daisy and Raven behind the building and into the pen with the six other dogs that had been boarded. The fenced-off area was a few hundred feet behind the building.

The floodlights that normally illuminated the grassy area were off. Whether from sabotage or fire, he couldn't be certain. The breeze carried the smells of wet dog, smoke and burning lumber. A few houses' worth of people came their way, forming a crowd on the sidewalks.

When he shifted to check on each animal, Alexis moved directly behind him, rapidly talking into the phone. The dogs in the pen had to be scaring her. "You don't have to stay here," he said softly.

She put one hand over the receiver. "Oh yes, I do. I tried to go out the gate, and two dogs almost managed to get past me." She shivered. "Marla says she's on her way. She wants to know if she should bring anything."

He shook his head. What they really needed were volunteers to bathe the dogs to get any potential soot out of their fur, house them and provide humidifiers to decrease the chance of suffering from the effects of smoke inhalation.

Thanks to Keri and Alexis, no animals had been harmed tonight. His heart sped up at the thought. It was too close, just as Alexis's brush with death on that cliff had been.

The fire was dying fast, thanks to the work of the firefighters behind them, but the remaining flames illuminated the approach of the chief and Jeremy. "Doc," the chief called out. "Need to ask some questions."

Alexis stiffened.

Nick regarded her. "Do I need a lawyer?"

"They probably just want to ask questions to start the investigation, but I'll be the first to tell you to get one."

For some reason the response hurt. "You wouldn't be my lawyer?"

"Not my field, remember?" She worried her lip. "Trust me. You wouldn't want me."

"Pretty sure I made the opposite point an hour ago." He realized it was the worst time to discuss it, but there was something about having his life's work go up in flames that put him in an argumentative mood.

"Nick, that was a completely different matt—"

"What can you tell us?" the chief interrupted. He stood just outside the pen.

Alexis spoke before Nick had a chance, relaying the details of what they'd seen and done.

Jeremy threw a thumb over his shoulder. "We found cement blocks up against the back door." He sent a tentative glance to Chief. "That's why Keri had to come out the front."

"Why would someone do that?" Chief asked.

"I was hoping you could tell me." Nick's voice raised an octave.

Alexis rested her hand on his forearm. Her touch simultaneously calmed and invigorated him. He took a deep breath and consciously relaxed his muscles.

"You have all the facts," Alexis told the chief, her voice steely. "I imagine you should be looking for the same person who cut my brakes."

Chief exchanged a glance with Jeremy. "Lexi, we can't jump to conclusions until we—"

"Investigate. Yes, I know. Surely you see this is arson." She gestured wildly to the burning building behind them. Unfortunately one of the dogs, Sugar, took the arm motion to mean *jump* and did so right in her face. Alexis squealed and spun, shoving her face into Nick's chest.

He wrapped his arms around her and pointed his finger down. "It's okay," he whispered. Sugar plopped on the ground, looking up, pleased she'd obeyed the command, and waiting for a treat. She wasn't the only one. Raven followed her example.

Nick tried not to enjoy the sensation of Alexis in his arms, especially as both Jeremy and the chief were glaring at him. He tried not to sigh aloud, but the burden of what lay before him in the days to come felt heavy enough to bury him alive. Was anyone on his side?

Alexis stiffened. Nick Kendrick's arms were around her, and her hands and face were pressed against his chest. She pulled away, her face hotter than the remaining blaze behind her. "Sorry." Her eyes searched for the dogs. The offending black Lab that had jumped in her face lay on the ground like nothing had ever happened.

Someone cleared his throat and coughed behind her. She whirled around to see the chief behind the gate, arms crossed over his chest. "I think it's time someone helped me out of here," she said.

Jeremy opened the gate and blocked the animals from escaping as she slipped out.

"You have an alarm system," the chief said to Nick. "I'm told Doc Finn never had one. Why did you feel the need to install it?"

"Doc Finn never had a sprinkler system, either," Nick answered coolly. "If I didn't have that, there would have been a lot of sorrow in this town. The practice needed some upgrades."

Alexis looked between the chief and Nick. It seemed like an odd thing to ask. Doc Finn had been in practice for over forty years. Nick adding such features was reasonable.

"Since I store pharmaceuticals, I need to take precautions, so I got the alarm system."

"Which pharmaceuticals were you worried about?" the chief volleyed.

Nick raised an eyebrow. "Tramadol, for one."

"What's that?" Jeremy asked.

"A pain reliever. It's narcotic-like but it isn't monitored like opiates, which can make it a target for some addicts."

Jeremy and the chief shared a knowing look. Alexis couldn't figure out why, though. It wasn't as if Nick was a drug dealer.

"Do you stock something called carfentanil?" Chief asked.

Nick's eyes went wide. "Elephant tranquilizer? No. I would have no need for that. I work with horses and cattle occasionally, but not anything of the size and weight to justify that."

Alexis studied the stances of the men. "What's going on? Why are you following this line of questioning?"

Jeremy's young face looked like he'd aged several years in the last day. "There was an overdose a couple days ago. Our EMTs gave three doses of Narcan." He turned to Alexis. "It's like an antidote for opioids, only it didn't work. We just got confirmation that the death was due to elephant tranquilizer."

Nick leaned forward. "Was it mixed with heroin?"

Chief lifted his head in surprise. "How did you know that?"

"My brother worked for the DEA. That combination of drugs seems to be one of the latest highs sought after and also one of the more dangerous. Even in school, when we had to handle carfentanil, we needed to wear protective gear. In its pure form, it can be absorbed through the skin or by inhalation." He shook his head. "It's ten thousand times more potent than morphine. They put a miniscule amount in the heroin. But even then, the risk of overdosing, of having a bad reaction…" His voice trailed off, laced with concern.

The chief's stance relaxed. "The DEA? Where's your brother stationed?"

"He's not. Drug runners killed him a couple years ago."

Alexis barely registered the noises in the background. Even the dogs seemed to know to quiet down and give Nick his space. So his brother had died trying to get lethal drugs off the street.

A loud crash shook the ground. The back half of the veterinary hospital's roof had collapsed. She wanted to cry for Nick. The strain on his face suggested that if one more thing went wrong, he would break.

"Doc Kendrick!" Marla, a woman Alexis recognized from church, rushed up in a rain jacket, baseball cap, T-shirt and polka-dot pajama pants. "We've got volunteers coming to take care of the animals. What else do you need me to do?"

Nick's eyes hardened. He pointed at the barely smoldering fire behind them. "Our main concern is smoke inhalation. Ask the volunteers to give the dogs baths and let them sleep inside, preferably with a humidifier." Marla's scrunched up face matched Alexis's confusion. "It'll help them cough up anything in their lungs," Nick added. "After that…well, we'll take it a day at a time."

The chief waved Nick to come out of the pen. Marla

took his place as four more women and three men rushed to the scene. Nick gave them a small wave of thanks, then stepped aside to let them take it from there.

"Doc, hold up." Marla spun around. "I found volunteers for all the animals we've boarded, but I didn't know anything about this young Lab. Any medical considerations before I find her a place to stay?"

"She comes with me," Nick said. Marla led Raven out of the pen with a leash someone had brought over. He accepted the leash and led her closer to the cops.

Alexis didn't understand why he wouldn't want to let a volunteer take care of her. Didn't he have enough to deal with as it was? Or did he think she wanted to take care of the dog? He would be sorely mistaken. "Is this because I haven't reached Theresa yet? I've left messages."

"Raven's a detection canine. Her nasal care will be a priority so her sniffing ability isn't hindered. Until we get word from Theresa, I'd prefer to keep an eye on her myself."

Nick joined the officers, but before the chief could say another word, Alexis rushed in. "Wait a second. Jeremy, why'd you even bring up elephant tranquilizers? Where is the silver Outback? I called you about the suspicious car, and you said you'd send someone. What happened?"

"Officer Sanders did a drive-by, Lexi. He didn't—"

"It's Alexis," she interjected.

The chief and Jeremy shared a conspiratorial look as if she was overreacting. Well, she'd tried to get people to call her by her real name since she'd been back. And after the night she'd had, it was the least they could do to acknowledge her by her legal, adult name instead of the nickname she'd had as a child.

"Okay, Alexis," Chief said slowly. "None of my men saw a silver Outback at the scene. We need to ask about the tranquilizer since Nick is a veterinarian and the only witness to the alleged drugs on—" he looked around for eavesdroppers "—the mayor's property."

"I don't see how that's relevant," Alexis said.

The chief leaned backward and swung forward as if gearing up to tell her off. Instead he just blew out a breath of frustration. "I'm not accusing the man of anything, Lex—Alexis. I'm just gathering information."

She would've taken a deep breath herself, but the wind had shifted and smoke tendrils were heading their way. "Well, how about gathering more information on the fire, then?"

Her mother had always told her she would make the perfect lawyer because the instinct to argue came to the surface in a heartbeat, but Alexis thought there was more to it than that. She gave in to the impulse when she advocated for someone, not only for the sake of debating. Nick tilted his head, studying her, but with no obvious emotion other than curiosity.

Chief raised an eyebrow. "Do you have more to tell me?"

"Yes. I saw a figure—a shadow running to the build…" She faltered. "Never mind. It was probably Keri running back inside to get the animals before someone blocked her in. And even if it was the person who barred the door and set the fire, I didn't see any identifying characteristics."

Though it did mean that whoever started the fire

saw Keri run back into the building before blocking her in. On purpose. Why would someone do that? Surely whoever did this didn't mistake Keri for Nick. While it was possible they thought Nick was still inside the animal hospital, why not wait for the girl to leave? Unless… Nick wasn't the target.

"What is it?" Nick put a hand on her shoulder. "You look as if you've figured something out."

"Chief, you said that there was a hit-and-run. Both Joe and Raven were inside that car, right? Raven was also inside my car when the brakes went out, and she was inside the animal hospital when the fire started. Maybe the arsonist wasn't trying to kill Keri or Nick. Maybe they were out for Raven."

Chief raised an eyebrow. "That's an awful lot of speculation without any facts."

Nick's face became animated. "Chief, you said yourself that Raven was going to be a gift that the town could never afford in the budget. In the next county alone, drug detection dogs sniffed out almost five million dollars in drugs within eight years. I know we're a small town, but we're also next to the interstate—The Corridor."

Jeremy's eyes widened. "We haven't looked at it from that angle."

Chief flashed an aggravated expression at Jeremy and shook his head. "That doesn't seem plausible to me. You're trying to give yourself hope that you're not in danger, which is understandable. But I think we're dealing with more than someone who has it out for a dog. I hate to break it to you, Lexi, but in the dark, you and Keri have the same build and hair length. No one has any reason to want to harm Keri. But if we assume you and Nick are targets and they thought you were heading into the vet hospital, it stands to reason they would think Nick was already inside."

Nick took a step to the side and looked at her profile. He sighed. "I'm afraid he's right."

Dread weighed down her bones. She looked into Nick's eyes but addressed Chief. "You're saying we're still in danger."

The chief rubbed his forehead. "Do you two have somewhere you could go for the night? Somewhere in town most people wouldn't assume you'd be staying?"

In other words, they needed to hide.

# SEVEN

Nick waited in the car as Alexis had suggested. He struggled to stay awake and probably wouldn't have succeeded if not for being keenly aware of how bad he smelled. Even his skin had the putrid scent of burnt plastic combined with wood and wet dog. Of course the last smell might have been due to the dog pressed up against his side in the backseat. At least she seemed to be breathing well.

Alexis opened the door at the back of the hotel. She leaned forward, a backpack looped over her shoulder, and looked both ways before she waved him to come toward her. He stepped out of her dad's car before grabbing the duffel bag of clothes and toiletries she had gathered for him at her parents' house before they'd left. By the time the firefighters and police were done with them, it'd been well past midnight.

Nick stepped through the entrance with Raven right by his side. He questioned whether he had the energy to make it through a shower before his head hit the pillow.

"I know the hotel receptionist from high school." She hustled him into an elevator and rapidly pressed the button to make the doors close. "She was willing to put our rooms under fake names."

"I'm pretty sure the button doesn't respond faster the more you press it."

She rolled her eyes. "But it makes me feel better."

Far be it from him to argue with that. He would do anything to feel better at the moment, but his problem was more physical than emotional. His entire body hurt from the cliff incident as well as the fire. He reckoned his emotions were too worn out to make themselves known.

Alexis's clothes and face showed the telltale signs of soot, the same as his, but somehow she still looked beautiful. "There's something I've been wondering about," he said.

She raised an eyebrow. "If after today you're wondering about only one thing, then something is wrong with you."

"No denying that." He smiled as the elevator jolted to a stop. "It's about you."

The doors opened and she stepped out into the hallway. "Oh?" She didn't slow her pace as she strode, glancing down at the numbers on the packet of keys she held and back up at the numbers listed on the doors.

"At the fire, you were quick to advocate for me." In his opinion, it hadn't gotten to the point of needing a defender, but he still appreciated the way she passionately took up his cause with the police. "It just made me wonder if you were reconsidering—"

Alexis stiffened and looked over her shoulder at him. "No." She shoved the key in the slot and waited for the light to switch to green. She turned the handle and opened the door. "I haven't changed my mind. I'm sorry I'm not up for going into more detail, but it's personal."

"I can honestly say that's the first time I've received the 'It's not you, it's me' line."

"You're welcome." She flashed a tired smile. "Everyone should hear that at least once in their lives. It's part of getting old."

"So you've experienced it?"

She looked at her shoes for a moment. "I plan on staying forever young." She kept her head down, but her eyelashes rose slowly until she met his gaze and smiled. She turned her hand over so he could take his keycard. "Good night, Nick."

He remained rooted to the floor as she gently closed the door. If he weren't in such an exhaustion-induced fog, he'd almost have believed she had flirted with him. Raven shook, her entire body resembling a giant spinning brush. What remaining droplets she had on her fur flung onto his exposed forearm, as if she was trying to tell him he was way off base.

It was enough to snap him out of his stupor. "Let's get both of us cleaned up and pass out." First order of business was to take his clothes and tie them up in a hotel laundry bag. He couldn't wait to smell something other than fire-tainted clothes and hair.

By the time he'd separately bathed and dried off himself and Raven, it was almost two in the morning. Raven had a short sneezing fit after her shower, which was probably the best thing for her after the smoke exposure. Nick examined her once more, struggling to keep his eyes open. Confident she didn't need any more treatment, he passed out the moment his head hit the pillow.

Sleep came in fitful bursts as he woke up multiple times after experiencing the horror of his business going up in flames all over again. He'd close his eyes and try to picture something nice, like the river flowing over rocks, but those dreams quickly morphed into a repeat performance of running with Alexis and Raven away from gunmen.

The moment six in the morning came, he gave up on trying to rest. He wouldn't get any answers about insurance until the holiday weekend was over. He wondered if there was an abandoned storefront that would serve as a makeshift practice. There would be so much to do next week. He needed a walk to clear his head.

Raven probably needed a break outside anyway. At least she seemed to have slept peacefully. Her breathing sounded normal, which was a relief.

He took the stairs to avoid other early risers. Using a back alley—the town seemed to have more alleys than streets—they walked to a drive-up coffee booth. The barista didn't mind and even gave Raven a dog treat. He was glad Raven had enjoyed a full meal before the fire.

He loved the small, laid-back town, and such a small gesture was an example of why. There would be a long journey ahead to rebuild his practice at the same time he was campaigning for mayor. The thought overwhelmed him enough that he put it out of his mind. With two lattes and breakfast sandwiches in his hands, he returned the way he'd traveled, on high alert for anyone who might be watching him. The dog seemed relaxed, though, all the way to the room.

Only when he felt certain he heard Alexis moving around did he knock on the connecting door. She wrenched it open. She was dressed in sweats herself, and her hair stuck up and out in every direction. Her wide eyes gazed at Raven. "Everybody okay?" She noticed the two cups in his hands. "My hero." She grabbed one and greedily sipped it before her face flushed. "I'm sorry. Did it matter which one I took?"

He'd yet to meet someone who needed coffee in the morning as badly as he did. All those late nights studying in veterinary school had conditioned him to need it before functioning, even before getting dressed in the morning. He supposed law school had a similar effect on her. "Either one." He grinned. "You can go back to sleep."

"No." She shook her head. "I was having a nightmare when you knocked."

Nick sobered. The noise he'd heard had been her thrashing in a nightmare? It served as a reminder that they needed to be proactive to get their lives back. He waved his hand at the breakfast sandwiches on the table in his room. "Since we both can't sleep…"

She left the connecting door open and eagerly sat down to eat.

He took a seat at the small desk on the opposite side of the room and pointed to the paper and pen. In small towns, sometimes an officer who had a knack for drawing would volunteer in a dual role as forensic artist, but to his knowledge, the Barings police wasn't that fortunate. "How about we try again to sketch the drug scout? Tell me everything you remember."

She swallowed and stared up at the ceiling. "He looked like an out-of-work cowboy."

Maybe this wasn't going to be as useful as he'd hoped. "I don't remember cowboy boots."

"No. They were brown work boots. But his stance, the faded jeans plus the green-and-brown flannel shirt made me think of it. Thin brown hair that was starting to recede emphasized his round face. No five-o'clock shadow, but he had stubble over his upper lip. I don't remember the color of his eyes, just that they were a little too close together and had nothing in them but coldness." Her voice shook slightly. She stared at the curtains but seemed lost in her memories.

If she thought about it anymore her fear might increase, so Nick broke in, "I think we remember him the same way. I can take it from here."

She stood and shook her head. "No. I think it would help if I could get him out of my mind. We should both try to draw our own versions, then compare notes. If we are in agreement, we can take it to the chief, they can put out an alert and maybe this whole thing will finally be over."

It wasn't a bad idea. "Only if you let me be the one to sign it."

"You want to take credit for my artwork?"

He ignored her attempt at a joke. "I don't want you to be a target anymore."

She shook her head. "Like it or not, we were both on that property. We are in this together. It's my fault you're even in this mess."

"I was the one who peeked in the gutters," he argued. As far as he could tell, no good would come if they focused on fault-finding.

She pointed at Raven. "You can thank her for the gutters tip." She held up the cup of coffee. "But I thank you for this." She shuffled to her side of the door but didn't close it.

Nick shut his eyes, trying to recreate fully his memory of the scout who'd started this whole mess. He sketched, erased and tried again. Minutes turned into hours. Raven's soft snores and the sound of the pen strokes were the only noises except for distant vacuuming down the hallway.

"Nick," Alexis cried. "This is horrible." She ran into the room and held up her phone. "Theresa called in the middle of the night. My Do Not Disturb setting automatically comes on at night, and I missed it!" She shivered. "Listen." She pressed the speaker button on her phone's voice mail feature.

Nick jumped up and went to her side, wondering how to comfort her as he listened.

"Alexis, something's happened." The woman hiccupped and sniffed. "We need to talk immediately. In person. I got your message. I think you might be in danger, honey." The crashing of small items and a shuffling of papers could be heard in the background. "Where are my stupid time cards?" The sound of glass smashing blasted through the phone speaker. Alexis flinched, even though it had to be the second time she'd heard it. The message abruptly ended.

Alexis bit her lip. "I'm worried something's happened to her."

Nick barely registered her words. The only thing that stuck in his mind was what Theresa had said on the message: *I think you might be in danger.*

"Let's go. You can call the police on our way."
He grabbed the dog and ushered Alexis out the door.

Alexis shoved the keys at Nick as her other hand
held the phone to her ear. "She's still not answering."
She looked at her phone and pulled up the number
Theresa had called from. "She used her office landline, not her cell, so we know she came back into
town. Let's start there." She dialed the police, rattled
off the address of the office and repeated the information to the dispatcher.

She directed him as he slowed at the front of the
storefront of the employment office. "Park in the
back." The side mirror showed an empty street behind them, but she didn't want to risk leading the drug
runners to Theresa's place.

Nick pulled into one of the spaces behind the strip
of local businesses. One building down, a sprinkling
of shattered glass from Theresa's employee entrance
was spread across the pavement. Alexis's heart jolted.
"Theresa." She shoved open the passenger car door
before Nick had shifted into Park.

"Alexis, wait!"

She couldn't wait. Theresa had called her. She'd
needed help, and Alexis had slept through it. She had
the good sense to pull her sweatshirt sleeve down over
her hand as she wrenched open the door. Unlocked.
Of course.

"Someone could still be in there," Nick hollered
as he caught up.

"Don't touch anything. If someone stole Theresa's stuff—" Her feet crunched on the broken glass
on the tile floor.

Straight ahead, Theresa's broken body lay in the middle of the floor on the cheap gray commercial carpet.

Alexis's throat closed, so tight and painful she could hardly breathe. Her legs refused to move forward.

"I'm calling for an ambulance." Nick passed her and crouched down at Theresa's side.

"Is she…?" Alexis couldn't speak her fear aloud.

He stood up, his face pinched. She knew the truth as he approached. She understood, but she couldn't believe it until he said it. Nick put his hand on her shoulder and turned her around.

"She wouldn't have wanted you to see her like that," he whispered.

Alexis choked on a sob as Nick led her outside the building and back to the car. "We need to wait for the police," he said softly. She left the car door open, her feet on the ground, as she sank onto the car seat and fought to hold the tears back. Raven climbed over the console and tried to rest her head on Alexis's shoulder.

The caring that came from an animal, of all things, was her undoing. The warmth helped the tears break. Nick reached around her to open the glove box and found a box of tissues. Her mom had always kept Dad's car well stocked.

Nick remained standing but put a hand on her shoulder. He opened his mouth as if to say something when sirens approached. Two officers she recognized from the mayor's property and one of the EMTs from last night barely gave them a second glance as they charged inside.

"H-how did…?"

Nick swallowed. "I'm not a—"

"Then give me your best guess. Please." She knew he wasn't a doctor, but he had eyes.

He avoided her gaze and crouched down. His hand moved to her wrist. "Did she have any medical problems?"

"Asthma."

He frowned. "Any legitimate medical reason to use a syringe?"

"No." Her breathing grew ragged. She shook her head. "No. Theresa was a health nut. What are you not telling me?"

One officer came out of the office and approached. "Were you the ones who called it in?"

Nick stood. "Yes, Officer." He explained about the voice mail Alexis had received, presumably so she wouldn't have to talk.

The officer looked over Nick's shoulder. "Could you save a copy of the message and send it to our main email address?"

"Of course." Alexis pulled her phone out and went through the motions as the officer rattled off the address. She blinked rapidly as the message sent, trying to force her mind to work properly. "What do you think happened to her?" she asked.

The officer shuffled his feet and looked out into the trees behind the parking spaces. "I can't say. There will be an investigation and a toxicology report. But, unofficially, it looks just like an overdose we had the other day."

Alexis hopped to her feet. Her heart jumped to her throat. "No. Theresa would never use drugs." She sought out Nick's gaze. "She wouldn't." She pointed at the door. "What about the broken window?"

"Like I said, there will be an investigation."

A cherry-red BMW pulled into the lot and parked roughly ten spaces down. Dr. Bill Tindale worked in the small clinic inside the final building at the end.

He got out of the car, frown lines etched on his otherwise handsome face. He spotted Alexis, and his eyes widened. A familiar face served as a balm at the moment. She waved at him, and he strode over. "Alexis, what happened?"

"It's Theresa." She poured out the story again. "Please tell them this wasn't an accident. Can you go in and tell—"

The officer held up a hand. "I'm sorry, Doctor. I can't let you—"

"I understand," Dr. Tindale said. He put an arm around Alexis's shoulders. "I'm afraid this isn't my area of expertise. But if there is anything I can do to help—"

It might've been her imagination or the grief, but it looked like Nick tensed. She didn't take time to analyze it, though. "Were you about to go into the clinic?"

He nodded and removed his arm. "Yes. I just wanted to catch up on some charts and paperwork."

She pointed over his shoulder in the direction of the dermatology clinic's employee entrance. "You have a security system. A security camera?"

"Yes, we do," he said eagerly as if just remembering it himself. He gestured toward the officer. "You're welcome to look through our footage." The officer seemed relieved and pulled out a notebook to write something down. Dr. Tindale reached for Alexis's hand

and gave it a gentle squeeze. "You have my number, Alexis. Don't hesitate to use it, okay?"

Her cheeks heated under the intense scrutiny. "Thank you… Bill." She'd never called him by his first name before, despite the many times he'd asked, but he was going to be the answer to catching Theresa's killer. He beamed and gave a gentlemanly nod before he walked back to his clinic.

"Okay, so we'll get the tape," the officer said, almost as if he was hinting for them to leave. Why wouldn't anyone acknowledge that this wasn't an overdose?

"Tell me this," Alexis said. "Why would a woman who drinks kale smoothies instead of coffee, eats carob instead of chocolate, and runs an air purifier in both her workplace and home ever choose to put drugs in her body?" She held up a hand and swallowed another sob threatening to overtake her. "No. If she died from an overdose, it was by force."

Nick put a hand on her back. "Maybe we should let them work." He said the words softly. "I'm sure Jeremy would be willing to give you updates if you asked him."

She whirled to Nick. "We're on the same page, though, right? This was murder. You heard the glass breaking at the end of the message."

"We can't offer any statements, ma'am." The officer looked as if he'd rather go back inside to the murder scene.

"Listen. She'd left on a romantic weekend with someone from town. The man, whoever she was dating, he might know something."

"You don't know who this man is?"

She deflated. "No. They were keeping their relationship discreet."

The officer didn't look convinced. The second officer stepped outside. "We found her landline and identification but no cell phone." He pointed at them. "Did you see a cell phone when you found the deceased?"

Alexis sucked in a sharp breath. The deceased? She had a name. Her hands fisted. This was her boss, her friend…

"No," Nick answered. "Other than the landline on her desk, I didn't see any phones." He pressed his hand at the small of Alexis's back and gently guided her to the car. "You have our phone numbers and names if you need us. Can we go?"

The first officer nodded and joined the second in conversation. How could they stand there as if nothing had happened? Nick closed the door once she was seated and walked around to the driver's side. As soon as he started the car, her stomach tightened, not appreciating that breakfast sandwich after all. "You didn't answer the question. Do you agree with me?"

"After the last twenty-four hours, I don't claim to know anything, but—" he turned the car in the direction of the hotel "—someone with asthma would've been at increased risk of overdose. I didn't know her, but I trust your opinion of her."

She pressed her back against the seat. His trust should've soothed her in some way. Instead, it just reminded her that her opinion of people couldn't be trusted. Could Theresa have been into drugs? No. Although Theresa had admitted to loneliness in the past. Maybe the new mystery man led her down the wrong path. The heart could be deceitful.

"So, are you and the doctor…?"

"Uh, no."

"Sorry. He just seemed…extra friendly."

"Well, it wasn't your imagination. He has been, and I've turned him down flat. Many times. I have no intention of dating anyone in town when I don't plan to be here permanently." Besides, she sometimes temped in his practice, and it seemed weird.

"Makes sense," he said drily.

"But Theresa was dating someone in town, and we need to find the guy. We need to get answers."

She watched Nick's profile. He remained stoic, without a nod of agreement. Why was she trying to include him? Theresa's death might not have anything to do with what happened to them yesterday, but it did involve drugs. "Is your number one agenda as mayor to pull drugs off the street?"

He blinked in surprise as he turned into the hotel parking lot. "Won't do any good if we're not helping people at the same time. At the bare minimum, I want a resource officer at the schools and some kind of community program to help users get the rehab and counseling they need."

Right now she wanted only justice. She wanted the dealers and runners to pay, to be punished. Nick said dealers had killed his brother. "Are you running for mayor for yourself or your brother?" The question slipped out before she could filter it.

He shrugged. "Does it matter?"

"Don't you want revenge?" She blinked rapidly, hot tears trying to escape.

A heavy sigh escaped him as he sagged and closed his eyes. "Not on good days."

"Is today a good day?" She hated the way these an-
tagonistic questions slipped out. She wanted to chase
this horrible sorrow and helpless feeling away. She
wanted him to get angry, be angry, with her so it
would hurt less.

He opened his brown eyes and looked at her with
compassion. Her bottom lip trembled. She couldn't
handle sympathy right now or she'd fall apart, without any hope of pulling herself back together again.

He laid a hand on her wrist. "No. It's not a good
day." His touch eased her swirling emotions just
enough that she could blink back the tears. He was
struggling, too, and didn't offer platitudes to gloss
over it. She should've felt guilty that she'd likely
pulled him down to her emotional level, but instead
she felt exceedingly grateful.

"The only thing I know to do," he said, "is to put
one foot in front of the other and do the next right
thing." He turned to stare into her eyes. "I don't go a
day without thinking of it."

A shiver went down her spine. Her hand twitched.
She was tempted to flip her palm over and hold hands
with him.

He removed his touch and leaned back in his seat.
"Doing something productive usually helps," he
said. "I would like to spend some more time trying
to sketch out what I remember about that scout guy,
but I don't want to ask that of you right now."

"No, that'd be good." He was right. They stepped
out of the car. She needed something constructive to
do, or she was going to go mad.

Nick walked Raven to a small grassy area while
Alexis waited at the hotel door. She needed to shower

and get dressed for the day. The temperatures were climbing fast, and the sweats were beginning to add to her discomfort. Every time she thought her life couldn't get worse...

"Did you want to call anyone?" Nick asked. "You can take the car and go to a friend's house while I stay at the hotel."

She shook her head. Because the truth was, she had no one. Not anymore. She'd been shunned by most of her lawyer friends back in Seattle, and she'd alienated everyone but Theresa when she'd come back to town. Even Theresa didn't know how she'd lost her job. She hadn't even asked.

The elevator opened on the second floor. Raven lifted her head and touched her snout to Alexis's hand. Normally she would have flinched and been annoyed at a dog's touch, but she didn't mind at the moment. Raven seemed to understand her emotions. It was probably a rare trait in a dog.

Shuffling behind Nick down the hall, she saw his spine stiffen. Raven made a guttural sound.

"What is it?"

"Call the police," he whispered.

She peeked around him. Her hotel door was slightly ajar. "Maybe it's housekeeping, or I didn't close it fully."

Nick tugged on the leash so Raven would step closer to him. "There's no housekeeping cart, and we both left the hotel through my door, not yours."

The moment he said it, she knew he was right. She dialed the number right away as they walked in the opposite direction of their rooms. "I think someone might be in my hotel room."

"Address?" the dispatcher asked.

Was she joking? There was only one hotel in their small town. She rattled off the name and cross streets.

"What's your room number? We've already received a call about two hotel rooms. A unit is already en route," the dispatcher said.

Alexis frowned. Two other hotel rooms? Her heart sped up. What was the likelihood after everything happening in the past twenty-four hours that two other rooms had been robbed? She looked up and down the hallway. All the other doors were closed. She clicked the phone off. Someone had called in their rooms, but only one of their hotel doors was ajar, which meant…

Nick's forehead wrinkled. "What?"

She strode back toward her room. "Something doesn't seem right." Her mind was so jumbled she couldn't put it into words. At the moment, she felt like she had nothing to lose.

"Alexis!" Nick warned her.

She ignored him and shoved past him.

"At least let me peek first."

"I have a weapon," he called out. Of course he didn't, but if people were in the room, it might make them think twice and leave from the other room.

She peeked around his shoulder from the doorway. The sunlight streamed through the gap in the heavy curtains, and the three lamps in the room were all on.

But not a single person was in the room.

She strode past him. The bed sheets were in disarray, exactly as she'd left them. Her backpack sat on the couch, open. The clothes inside looked jumbled, not folded as she remembered. She strode to the desk. The drawing she'd started to sketch was missing.

Clarity hit her over the head. She spun around to tell Nick to check his room, but he was too busy being led by Raven, who was sniffing frantically at the dresser. Raven barked and sat down.

As a drug-sniffing K9 in training, it could mean only one thing. "We've been set up."

# EIGHT

Nick grabbed a couple of tissues and used them to prevent leaving fingerprints as he pulled the drawer open. Two small bags of white powder and two syringes sat neatly inside. He suspected it was several hundred dollars' worth of heroin. He stepped backward. "I can't believe this."

"Please don't tell me it's what I think it is." Alexis ran to his side and put a hand over her mouth.

Raven put her nose to the carpet and pulled him through the connecting door into his own hotel room. He let her lead until she sniffed near the refrigerator and stood on her hind legs, her nose up in the air. She sat down and sneezed.

Odd. He opened the minifridge. Nothing.

"We need to get out of here, Nick." Alexis stood in the doorway with her backpack slung over her shoulder. She looked past him to his desk and strode across the room. "Your sketch is gone, too."

Great. Hours of work, stolen. Nick pulled open the microwave. Nothing there. Maybe Raven had lost her touch, but she lifted her head again as if pointing. "If someone is framing me, I'd like to know exactly what I supposedly did."

On the countertop, he used the tissues again as he opened the lid of the coffeemaker where the water was to be poured. A clear glass vial about three inches long was propped up on its side. He reached for it and stopped. He leaned forward and squinted at the printed label. "Carfentanil." A wave of nausea rushed through him at the sight. He blew out a breath and closed the lid softly. "We need to go into the hall."

In veterinary school, he'd handled the drug only once. And even then, they wore protective outer coverings, masks and goggles. One drop of pure, undiluted carfentanil, either inhaled or touched had the potential to kill multiple people. He'd heard that there was a new trend for drug dealers to lace heroin with fentanyl, another dangerous and potentially deadly opioid, but carfentanil was an entirely differently matter. "Call the police."

"I did, remember? They're already on their way, but they're not coming to help us, Nick. I have a feeling all these little presents we're finding are connected to Theres—" Emotion overtook her voice. She shook her head. "Let's go." She picked up the duffel bag of her dad's clothes, zipped it and threw it at him.

He lunged for it and caught one of the handles with his left hand. "Careful! If that had hit the coffeemaker, we'd have much bigger problems. At least the vial is closed. We should just tell the police what happened."

She raised an eyebrow. "Do you think you're going to have a chance at winning the mayor's office if you've been arrested for drug possession?"

"But I'm not possessing it! And I think it'll hurt my campaign if I leave."

She flicked her index finger at him. "You have the means and the opportunity."

"No motive!"

"No? Seems to me you tried to pin this on our current mayor?"

"I did no such thing."

"I believe you, but I'm trying to show you what could happen." She shoved her index finger toward her collarbone. "And I'm a lawyer who has been working entry-level jobs and probably needs to sell this heroin for the money. See? I'm telling you, they've got enough to hold us. I say we be proactive and clear our names. Let's at least go somewhere we can sketch out this scout picture and then regroup. I'm not waiting around for them to decide we should be arrested. If they come to that conclusion, hopefully I'll have found something to clear our names by then."

Her reasoning was attacking his first instinct to stay and reasonably plead his case to the local authorities. She strode past him and opened the door. "I'm going with or without you. I need to know who is behind this, for Theresa's sake."

He followed her to the stairway. "At the very least, will you call the police and be up front about what we found? Pass on the strict instructions on how to handle the carfentanil. They could die packaging the evidence if they decide to open it and take a sniff."

She eyed him for a second. "You can talk to them in the car."

They raced downstairs and out the back door. "What I don't understand is how someone found us," he said. "We were very careful to make sure no one followed us here." He barely made it inside the vehicle before she turned the key in the ignition. She sped through the parking lot and turned into a back alley.

Gravel pummeled the bottom of the car, making rattling noises as she drove. "Two thoughts come to mind," she said. "Someone might've recognized my parents' sedan in the parking lot." She shook her head. "But that seems very unlikely to me. It's been in the garage for months, and they don't so much as have an air freshener hanging from the mirror. No identifying factors unless someone has the resources to look up license plates easily."

"The mayor makes that a possibility."

"Nick, you're starting to sound like a broken record. The chief isn't the mayor's puppet. More likely, my high school reunion in the lobby was cause for gossip, despite asking my so-called friend to keep it quiet. In this town, it's hard to keep a secret." She inhaled and shook her head. "I should've known."

Nick wondered if she'd had secrets of her own spread through town before. He didn't come from a small town, but he knew the same could be true of the little communities within cities, especially in a college setting.

He knew from experience, and he never wanted to be the source of that kind of gossip again.

She took a sudden turn, and her eyes focused on the rearview mirror. The force of her turn sent Raven into his lap. He barely kept his head from hitting the side window. "Do you know where you're going?"

"The only place where no one would think to look."

"And that is?"

"Raven's home."

That would mean going to the handler's house. "The police said Joe's in intensive care in Boise."

She nodded. "I still have the key from when I picked up Raven."

"That's probably a good idea. I imagine Raven is pretty hungry by now."

Alexis paled. "I hadn't thought of that. I'm such a horrible dog sitter."

She turned into another alley and barreled past trash cans and bushes until she turned into a small carport and slammed on the brakes. The moment the car was still, Nick moved to check on Raven's stitches. "Good," he murmured.

She opened the door for him. "Come on. I don't want to be out in the open long. I'm sure no one is looking for us yet, but neighbors will take notice if we're not careful. If the rumor mill starts operating, we'll be in trouble."

"I have nothing to hide." He stood up straight. "And I'm not going to start acting like I do."

Alexis stepped up to the back door and unlocked it. Raven tugged on the leash, and Nick let her lead the way. Sure enough, she ran for the full food dish set beside the washing machine.

He closed the door behind him. In the modest but clean home, the room adjoining the laundry room was filled with dog toys and training tools. Alexis made a beeline to the living room, where she found a desk and pulled out papers and pens. "We might not have much time."

"We haven't called the police yet," Nick said.

She took out her phone and pulled up Jeremy's

contact information. "I think I'd rather text him right now than give him a chance to tell me to come in."

Nick looked over her shoulder as she typed:

I called the police when I saw my hotel room was broken into. We spotted planted drug paraphernalia in our hotel rooms and got out of there to let police handle it.

"Only a lawyer would type out *paraphernalia* in a text."

She eyed him. "Do you want to do this?"

Nick tried not to smile at her response. The day had been filled with sorrow and stress. He needed to control his coping instincts to deflect and joke around. Especially since he enjoyed teasing her entirely too much. He dictated the important pieces of information as she texted:

Check the coffeemaker but wear protective goggles and gloves. We haven't touched any of it.

Her phone buzzed right after she pressed Send.

Where are you now?

She clicked the phone off. "I'm not going to give him a chance to tell me something I don't want to hear."

His gut turned to stone. She'd shut the phone off on a cop.

She gestured to the dining room table. "I think we should get drawing."

His nerves were shot. He rummaged in the cabinets until he found a drinking glass and got himself some water. Surely Raven's handler wouldn't mind if he did that. When this was all done, he might even go down and visit the guy in the hospital.

At the moment, it felt like this nightmare would never be finished. He turned around to face Alexis and leaned against the sink. Maybe if they understood why someone would murder her boss, then they would have a clue who planted evidence in their rooms. "Why would someone want to hurt Theresa?"

Alexis let her head drop so that her hair covered her face. At the sound of a sniff, he filled another glass of water and brought it to her. She drank greedily and wiped the gathering tears from her eyes. "I have no idea why anyone would want to."

She looked on the edge of collapse, but her determined glare made it clear she wouldn't be taking a rest. He picked up the pen and began sketching again. She followed his example. He took extra care to make it look more like the beady-eyed man who had started this mess and less like a turtle.

Minutes passed with only the sounds of swiping pens on the paper. Alexis straightened and flicked her hair back over her shoulder. Her drawing captured the essence of the man they'd seen. He pushed his paper closer so that they were side by side.

"You got his nose and face shape better," she remarked.

"But you got the eyes and mouth exactly right." He passed over his sketch, and they worked for another hour, combining their two sketches and making small changes until they both agreed they had it right.

He stood up, his back tight, and stretched his arms toward the ceiling. "I think that's the best we're going to do."

"Agreed. I'll send it in." She turned her phone's power back on, and it vibrated like crazy. Notifications of text messages and voice mails flashed on her screen. "I'm going to ignore those for a moment." She aimed the camera's phone at their artwork and snapped a photo. "Sending this to Jeremy."

The phone buzzed again. She stared at it. "He's calling. Should I answer it?"

It'd been only a couple of hours, but Nick was ready to stop hiding. The lack of sleep from the night before was catching up with him. He desperately wanted a nap, and the couch in the living room looked inviting, especially with Raven asleep on the rug in front of it. Sleep often helped him process things, and after the past couple of days, he needed a whole lot of processing. "Yes. Take the call."

She nodded and pressed the speakerphone.

"Alexis, where'd you get this photo?" An older man's voice came through loud and clear.

"Chief?" Her eyebrows rose. Apparently the chief had used Jeremy's phone. "Are you referring to the sketch of the drug scout I sent in?"

"I'm referring to the man I found dead from an apparent overdose twenty minutes ago. They appear to be one and the same."

Nick grabbed the edge of the chair to steady himself. The scout was dead? It seemed highly unlikely that the scout would die from an overdose. Usually those guys didn't touch the merchandise so they could be used as chase bait without charges worse than a traffic violation.

Nick leaned over and spoke into the phone. "Did you get the scout's phone? Could you tell us if he sent our photograph to anyone else? You could figure that out, right?"

The hope that the danger might all be over, that he could begin to rebuild his practice without having to look over his shoulder, filled him with hope.

"Mr. Kendrick is with you, then." Chief Spencer sighed. "Why don't you come in, Lexi, and I'd be glad to discuss everything with both of you."

Alexis pursed her lips and frowned. "Okay." She hit the End Call button. "Soon," she added. Her eyes steeled. "If the scout is dead, then why would they plant those drugs in our room? We can't identify anyone else."

"Maybe because we spotted the drugs at the mayor's house? We're still a threat."

She worried her lip. "Perhaps...but no, that still doesn't make sense to me. The mayor isn't going to get charged with anything. The drugs weren't there when the police arrived."

Nick stared at the ceiling. "Maybe Theresa's killer knew that once an investigation happened, it would become clear that it was murder and not an overdose."

"Then they would want to misdirect the police. Frame someone." She leaned forward. "What if the scout didn't willingly overdose? What if he was killed by the same thing that was sitting in our hotel room?"

He groaned. "Carfentanil."

She began pacing the room. "Why would the killer want to take out the scout in the first place?"

"Easy. We spotted him, which made him a risk to their operation and expendable. Plus, the killer could've seen the sketches in our room when he planted the drugs. Maybe he realized we were getting close."

She pivoted on her foot and faced him. "So why frame us?"

"Somehow they think we're still a risk. Maybe we've seen something else or—"

"—or might figure something out that they don't want us to know. I think we need to start by finding Theresa's mystery man."

"Won't the police do that?" Nick asked.

"Not if they take the easy way out and focus on the overdose theory. You said yourself that it looks like an overdose. They won't act on anything else until an autopsy. It'll take time for them to figure out it was murder. Thankfully, we're not waiting in a prison cell on possession charges while they puzzle through it." She crossed her arms over her chest. "The only way they know there is a mystery man is that I told them. Are they going to believe me after I had drugs in my hotel room?" She shook her head. "Theresa didn't want the whole town to know she was involved with someone local."

"It sounds like you knew her well. You must have some idea who she was seeing."

She shook her head mournfully. "No, but I have an idea of where to start looking."

Alexis reached for the leash but didn't see Nick's outstretched hand until their fingers bumped over the nylon. Heat rushed up her arm, and she yanked it back.

"Probably a better idea for you to take her." The view from the window showed nothing but bushes, trees and houses. "It's clear. I'll drive."

She drove in silence, taking a roundabout way to Theresa's house to make sure they weren't being followed. It was pretty easy as there weren't many cars on the road. Anyone who hadn't traveled for the holiday weekend was probably at the End of Summer celebration happening at the park on the outskirts of town.

She took the closest alley to get to the backside of Theresa's house without using the street. Like many of the older houses in town, Theresa had a carport instead of a garage. The house next door belonged to a family Alexis knew went out of town for every holiday weekend. She parked the car in their carport just in case the police drove by and wondered why there was a car at Theresa's house.

Nick clicked his tongue and Raven stayed close as they walked together. Nick's stomach growled so loudly that Alexis flinched. His sheepish grin almost gave her the giggles.

"Sorry," he said. "We missed lunch."

Judging by the colors in the sky and her hunger pangs, they were getting close to missing dinner, as well. They reached Theresa's back door, and Alexis stuck her hand into the flowerpot to retrieve the extra key, but her fingertips found only loose soil. She took a knee to make sure she was looking in the right place.

Nick touched her shoulder. "Alexis," he whispered. "I think someone is already in there."

"What? Who?"

He shrugged and shook his head.

Her skin electrified as all her senses heightened.

Who, other than the police, would be in Theresa's house? She straightened and tiptoed to the side window. A lone lamp was on, and a shadow crossed the room. "Not the cops," she whispered.

A guttural sob seeped through the thin windowpane. She met Nick's alarmed expression. "Someone is hurting in there." Nick grabbed the doorknob, and it turned easily.

"Wait," she cried. Raven and Nick rushed ahead of her.

She followed him inside, several paces back. Nick's spine stiffened as he reached the entrance to the living room. Alexis quickened her pace until she could look around him.

There, in the middle of Theresa's faded navy couch, Mayor Gerald's shoulders shook over the teddy bear clutched in his hands as he cried.

"You?" The word slipped out of her mouth before she could stop herself.

Gerald startled. His mouth hung open as tears ran down his cheeks. Confusion clouded his features. "Lexi?"

She pushed past Nick and Raven to face him. "You were her mystery guy?" She tried to recall everything Theresa had said about him. "You?" she said again. He was the last person she could imagine with Theresa.

Gerald leaned forward and pulled out a tissue from the box on the coffee table. He wiped his eyes. "I've known her forever. I've always—" He choked on his words and took several deep breaths. "She was the love of my life."

"Do the police know?" Nick spoke up behind her.

Gerald shook his head. "They can't help. I never should've taken—I—" His bottom lip wavered.

The renewed sorrow of losing Theresa washed over Alexis. She fought the tears back. "She didn't die of an overdose." She steeled her voice.

Gerald's head dropped. "I know."

"You had heroin on your property," Nick said.

Gerald raised an eyebrow but didn't make eye contact. He closed his lips and shook his head. "You should go," he whispered.

Fury swirled in her gut and threatened to be unleashed. This man knew Theresa hadn't died of an overdose but admitted it in such a nonchalant way? She wouldn't stand for it. "She was my friend. I want answers!"

"Well, you can't have them," Gerald shouted back.

Raven growled and appeared at her side. Nick put a hand on her arm. "Maybe we should have the police ask the questions, Alexis."

"That's a bad idea," Gerald said. He leaned back into the couch cushions, staring at the teddy bear still in his hands. "We were perfect for each other. I got her this in Boise before…" His voice trailed off, but he smiled sadly at Alexis. "We felt like kids again. She loved it."

In the distance, slamming doors could be heard. Gerald frowned. "She should've never died." His eyes lifted to meet Alexis's. "She wouldn't want you to be hurt, too. Go," he said.

Alexis turned to Nick in confusion. Nick's forehead scrunched, and he rushed to the front window. "Call the police. We've got men with guns."

"The cops won't make it in time." Gerald pointed

to the left. "Go out the old back door. The one in the guest room."

"But our car is—"

"They'll have already seen it. Go. It opens right into the bushes. Most people don't even know it's there."

The house used to be smaller before she renovated it, but Alexis didn't remember an old back door in there. "But you—"

"They won't hurt me, but I can't protect you. Go. For Theresa's sake, just go."

"Oh, is that so? Why won't they hurt you?" Her veins grew hot as her heart rate sped up. "Maybe because you're the ring leader of the drug operation?"

"Where's your truck?" Nick pressed. He had a phone pressed to his ear.

"Too far away for you to reach," Gerald responded with an eerie calm.

Nick spoke into the phone. "There are gunmen roaming the neighborhood." He listed the two closest cross streets and hung up.

"We don't have enough answers to go to the police yet," she told Nick.

"If they arrest these guys, maybe we don't need them." He tugged on her arm. "I have a feeling we should listen to Gerald, though, and get out of here while we have a chance. Come on."

She heard shouts outside and through one of the windows could see men approaching the car in the neighbor's carport, rifles in hand. The mayor didn't even move a muscle. "Just tell me this," she said. "If you loved her, why'd you give Theresa heroin? Even if I believed she wanted to get hit up—which I don't—

you would've had to have known she had asthma. You meant to kill her." They couldn't leave without a single answer. They'd be back to square one.

"I didn't. It wasn't me." The mayor closed his eyes and leaned his head back. "Right now, keeping her friends alive is all that matters. Just leave."

She gritted her teeth. She wanted to grab him by the shoulders and shake him until he told her who was behind Theresa's death.

Raven whined, and Nick grabbed Alexis's hand. His touch grounded her, and she knew she had to press past the swirling emotions and just stay alive. *For Theresa's sake.* Her tears threatened to escape. She focused on Nick's hand holding hers, reminding her to stay in the present moment.

He pulled her through the hallway and ran toward the first bedroom.

"No." She led him in the opposite direction. "That's her room." She couldn't bear to see Theresa's room without her in there. She pulled him to the guest room that she had stayed in once.

Nick ran for the first door he saw. It turned out to be a closet. "She's moved the bed," Alexis said. She pointed to where the bed used to be. The floral canvas that had hung above it was no longer there, either. The wall was covered with the same white vertical paneling as the rest of the room, but she realized she could see the outline of a very low door. It would have been covered by the canvas and headboard that had once been there.

Nick twisted the knob and had to push with some force before the door shoved open directly into hedges. No wonder Theresa kept it covered up. It wasn't a very practical place to have a door. Gerald had probably used it to visit Theresa while keeping their relationship a secret.

Nick couldn't open the door all the way, but Gerald had been right. It left them about one foot of space to squeeze outside. Nick took a step down onto the ground. Raven and Alexis quickly followed. She heard men running but could see no one. The foliage was too thick for them to hide inside the bushes, but if they were willing to endure some prickly branches, they could slide in between a set of them into the neighbor's yard. It was their only chance.

A man rounded the corner holding a rifle. Nick launched himself at the man, shoving the barrel up into the air. Raven's leash fell from his hand, but the dog stayed put.

The sound of a gunshot filled the air. A screech wrenched from her throat as she flinched, her hands over her head. Nick punched the man in the chin. The guy swung the barrel toward Nick's head. He evaded just enough that the rifle swished through the air half an inch over his forehead. Nick used the advantage to jab a fist into the guy's stomach and shove him backward.

Alexis didn't stand around and wait for the gunman to get back up. She dove through the bushes with Nick and Raven on her heels as the sound of another gunshot filled the air.

The sting from the scratching branches was hard to ignore, but she pumped her arms harder as she ran through the next backyard. Another gunshot sent her ducking. So far the only thing they'd accomplished was letting the rest of the drug ring know their location.

Within seconds, more gunmen would be on their way. Her first instinct was to hide behind the gas grill on the neighbor's patio and wait, but she knew if they did that, they would be dead meat. On either side of the yard was a hedge, but a five-foot-high cedar fence outlined the back border.

The men shouted at each other to surround the area.

Her breathing escalated. They were trapped.

# NINE

Nick grabbed her hand and pulled her around the corner of the house and into a tight space between the wall and a freestanding shed. Raven stayed close to Alexis, despite the leash dragging on the ground. He picked it up and they all hid in the tiny, dim spot.

"So, what's the plan?" she whispered.

"What do you mean?" He spoke into her hair. It smelled like the hotel shampoo, with the faint scent of vanilla and sugar cookies. It was enough to make his stomach roil with hunger again. "This is the only idea I've got. I'm hoping they think we went through the other hedge and kept running."

"How is this any different than when we started? At this rate they can find us in ten seconds."

"We're outnumbered with nowhere to go," Nick said. "Do you have any better ideas?" Raven sat on her haunches and stuck her nose in the air. Her ears twitched and her hackles rose. "See that? It means help is on the way."

She squinted. "What?"

A half second later, sirens could be heard. Alexis looked momentarily impressed until she saw the smug grin Nick knew he sported. "Let's hope the gunmen hear it, too, and start running before you get all smug."

The sound of panting and quick footsteps approached. Whoever they were, they had to be on the other side of the bushes. He held up a finger for a moment until he felt certain they'd kept running.

"Attack," Alexis whispered to Raven.

Raven tilted her head.

"Go get 'em, girl." She shoved her finger in the direction they'd come.

The dog scratched her ear with her back paw.

Alexis huffed. "Shouldn't she attack?"

He shrugged. "It's possible she hasn't or won't be trained to do that. I only knew about her health." Their shoulders touched as they leaned against the side of the house. Tight spaces made his skin crawl. Raven sat on his shoes and leaned her body into his legs as if she was prepared to take a nap. He gave her leash a small tug to keep her upright in case they needed to run. The sirens grew closer.

Alexis shook her head. "I'm not ready to go into police custody. I'll talk to them on the phone, but once I step into the station, I won't get a chance to find out who killed Theresa. Besides, Gerald is clearly involved in this. Who's to say we won't be in more danger once we're at the station?"

She had a point. "You're the one that thought the mayor wasn't in the pocket of the police. I agree with you now."

"After it's clear he's involved? What's your proof they're not?"

He shrugged. "No proof, just a feeling."

"Feelings are misleading."

That was also true, but he didn't want to dissect or think about it any longer. They needed a plan. In his mind, it was more important to focus on proving their innocence. "Do you know how long it takes them to run things for fingerprints?"

"I'm a lawyer, not a cop."

Someone yelled over a megaphone, "Put your hands up or you risk being shot." A gunshot sounded and Alexis flinched. It seemed to have come from the opposite direction of the police car. "I hope Jeremy is okay."

An unbidden spark of jealousy flew through Nick at the caring tone she used for the officer. He wouldn't let himself think about it now.

"We have to get out of here." She scooted past him and chanced a look around the corner of the shed. "How high do you think that back fence is?"

Gunshots in the distance accompanied her question.

He grimaced. Scaling fences wasn't exactly on his wish list for the day. Every muscle in his body still hurt from yesterday's events. He fought against rolling his eyes or arguing and peeked around the shed to see for himself. "Guessing five feet. At least it's cedar. Won't be as slippery or flimsy as vinyl."

She nodded. "If you can help me and Raven get over that back fence, I think I can get us somewhere safe."

Getting Raven over could be a problem. It would take all of his strength to lift the dog to that height to help her clear the fence. "It'll work only if you go over the fence first, and you'll have to get the dog down on the other side."

He was a grown man, a professional and a potential mayor who had been driven into hiding behind sheds and jumping fences. If he could have convinced Alexis to turn herself in to the police and trust God to be their defender, then he would have. But it was obvious she'd made up her mind, and he wouldn't let her go off on her own when he knew the drug trafficking ring was out to kill her. And the current mayor was… well, Nick wasn't sure what the man was doing, but he couldn't deny the possibility that Gerald was the one who had tried to frame them.

Gunshots sounded again. Obviously the gunmen weren't going to surrender to the police without a fight. Unless there were more police officers in the vicinity than usual, he felt certain that the gunmen would outnumber them.

The sky had turned a dark blue-gray and the stars were just starting to become visible. Day was turning into evening before his eyes. How could that be possible? Alexis's stomach growled as if in proof.

Alexis eyed him. "What? It's past my dinnertime, too." She blew out a breath.

A loud bang erupted, and sparks of blue and red filled the dark sky in the distance. It must be the practice set of fireworks before the End of Summer show that would start in a few minutes. He hoped the entire town was there and safe from the gunfight erupting behind them.

"When you hit the fence, jump vertically. Grab the top, but use your legs to climb the fence. All you need is one heel or knee to get over. Then you can twist and roll the rest of the way."

She blinked. "Okay." She pointed at Raven. "Do

that 'stay' command thing with her." She noticed the hesitation that must've been evident on his face. "When I make it over, run. I promise I'll be waiting to catch her on the other side. Let's go."

He nodded. He didn't feel ready. He held his hand out and firmly spoke. "Stay."

Alexis peeked around the shed and took off running. Raven's foot shoved off Nick's shoe as she launched after Alexis like a rocket. Nick groaned and charged after them both.

A gunman stepped out of the shadows on the other side of the house and aimed what looked like a sawed-off shotgun at her. The moon reflected off something near the grill. Nick grabbed what turned out to be the grill brush and flung it at the gunman. The metal edge hit the man's temple, but the gun still went off.

A bullet splintered the top of the fence right next to where Alexis had been half a second ago. She shrieked but managed to fling herself over the fence. Raven jumped over in a beautiful arc, the leash sailing behind her, proving she didn't need anyone to hoist her up.

Nick sucked in a sharp breath. That had been too close. They couldn't back down now.

Hearing the gunman behind him reloading, he vaulted across the yard before the man could take aim again. He launched himself sideways through the other bordering bushes. The branches slashed against his face and arms, much more painful than the first set of hedges, but he managed to get through. The yard resembled Theresa's except there was more furniture.

"Nick!" Alexis screamed from somewhere over the fence.

Nick didn't take time to answer. He didn't want the gunman to be able to zero in on his voice. Another gunshot and a scream told him the man had tried to aim at the sound of Alexis's voice instead.

Nick jumped, placed his hands on top of the fence, swung himself over and barely missed landing on Raven.

Alexis stood next to her. "Follow me."

Nick pumped his arms, careful not to pass her because she seemed to know where she was going. He leaned down and scooped up the middle of Raven's leash, picking up a handful of gravel with it. The grit stung underneath his fingernails, but he couldn't afford to slow down.

Alexis glanced down at Raven. "So she didn't want to obey and stay. I can see why she's still in training."

"Or maybe she just figured out who was really the boss," he said. Alexis might not want to admit it, but Raven acted as if she'd decided Alexis was her owner.

Fireworks hit the night sky, causing Alexis to flinch and shriek a little each time. Raven lifted her head up with each gallop but didn't bark or shake at the blasts and booms. It was becoming hard to recognize which booms came from guns and which from pyrotechnics. "Try not to make noise," he said, huffing his words.

Her eyes seemed to light up, reflecting another set of bursts in the sky. "I'm not doing it on purpose." She pointed to the left. "I know that home. I used to babysit for them. They never miss a fireworks show. It'll be empty." They ran to the porch, and she kicked back the mat to reveal a key. He looked over his shoulder to make sure the coast was clear as she opened the door and they slipped into the darkened house.

A hiss sounded and Raven responded with a bark. "Shh," Alexis responded. "It's just their cat. It's old. It won't hurt you, dog. We'll be right out of your hair, Snookums. Just passing through." She spoke in such soft, soothing tones, Nick felt his own spine relax a little.

He remained still until his eyes adjusted. Her footsteps echoed throughout the house, but he worried that if he tried to follow, he'd smash into something valuable. A moment later he could see her form down the hallway. She stood next to the back door, where a sliver of light came through the curtain.

"I don't know about you," she said, "but I'd rather avoid jumping a fence again. Follow me, but don't let the cat out."

He reached her at the door. "You sure it wouldn't be better to stay indoors for a bit?"

"Trust me. Come on." They slipped back outside as the fireworks increased in frequency in the fully darkened sky. In the distance, they could hear whoops and hollers.

Alexis closed the door behind him. He couldn't see details, but judging by the trellises and inverted cone shapes in long rectangular boxes in front of him, he imagined the owners gardened a lot. Alexis walked down a set of cement stairs to what looked like a cellar door.

"They told me I could come by anytime to pick up some of their produce." She used the same key from the front and shoved the heavy door open. "I never intended to take them up on it until today."

She waited until they were inside before she pulled a string. A lone lightbulb illuminated the shelves filled with glass jars. In the middle, a long countertop held baskets of fresh veggies awaiting a rinse from the industrial-sized sink sticking out of the right wall.

Alexis took a lone sugar snap pea out of a basket and shoved it toward him. "Am I wrong or did you think that Gerald was telling the truth about Theresa?" She put one hand on her hip as she waved the vegetable at him. "Because it seemed to me that you could've helped me press him until he told us what we needed. It's obvious that he's behind the entire thing. The drugs on his property had to be his."

Nick shrugged. "I'm not so sure."

"Why is that?" Her eyes narrowed.

He searched through the basket for snap peas without any indentions. "I didn't think we were going to get any more out of him. He seemed truly sorrowful." Nick strode to the sink to rinse the veggies, and Alexis followed close behind him.

"Yeah. From guilt. He shouldn't be able to live with himself." She scrunched up her face.

"I don't believe he killed her." Nick turned around and chewed on a pea. The taste just made him wish he had hummus nearby, but his stomach was happy to have any food.

"I'll ask you again. What makes you so sure?"

He couldn't help but smile. "I know I get argumentative when I'm hungry, but you…"

Her shoulders dropped a bit. "I admit I can get carried away."

"It's what makes you a good lawyer."

Her eyes lifted to meet his. "*Made* me a good lawyer."

He tilted his head. "There has to be a story behind that." He'd learned over the years that if he waited long enough, both people and animals would show him what they were hiding. Judging by her stance, Alexis was hiding something.

She pursed her lips. "Back to Gerald."

Clearly he hadn't earned her trust yet. He sighed. "Gerald struck me as a man who was genuinely in love."

Her eyes widened, and she took a step back. "Have you ever been in love?"

Alexis fought the urge to cover her mouth with her hand. The question came out before she could stop it. She'd lost control. Her emotions were more wild and rampant than they'd ever been, even when she'd been disbarred.

She wanted justice. She wanted truth. And she couldn't make herself take back the question to Nick, for some reason.

His raised eyebrows dropped and his lips formed a slanted smile. "Seems like kind of a personal question."

"We're on the run together. I don't see how you can get any more personal."

He nodded. "Fair enough. There have been plenty of times I wondered if I was falling in love, but in the end…no. I don't think I've ever been in love. Romantic love, anyway." He held out his hands. "So, I guess you're right not to trust my opinion of Gerald." His smile warmed her core, and she wished they'd stayed outside in the cool air. He stepped closer. "So now that I've answered your question, I would like you to answer mine."

She'd walked right into that one. It's what happened when she let emotions rule her mind instead of pure logic. "You want to know why I haven't been practicing law."

He shrugged. "When you're ready to tell me."

Oh, he was good. She found herself really wanting to open up at that very moment.

"Right now," he said, "I want to know if you have a history with Jeremy."

A snort threatened to escape. That was the last thing she ever expected him to ask. "I guess you could say we have a history. I changed his diapers when I was eight years old. I was a mother's helper. I worked for a couple dollars an hour and the occasional basket of free homemade cookies. Jeremy comes from a big family."

Nick looked pleased. "Just like you," he said.

She blinked, unable to process her feelings because she was too busy having to correct him. "I'm an only child."

"Seems like most of this town is your family."

At one time, she would've heartily agreed and been proud of it. Now she felt like an outsider. It was her own doing, but she couldn't focus on that. She looked toward the door. "I think we have a couple of hours before they'll be back from the festival. We could wait here to make sure the police caught the gunmen."

"Then what?" He stepped closer. His hand rested on the countertop, near hers.

Her index finger twitched. It'd helped when he

had grabbed her hand back at Theresa's house. It'd grounded her emotions and kept her mind on the present. But most of all, it had comforted her. She closed her eyes. "I need time to process, to focus, to pray." While it was true, wasn't that what she'd been saying the entire past year about the Seattle incident?

Before she could change the subject, Nick's hand slid on top of hers, his fingertips squeezing ever so slightly. "Lord, we need Your wisdom. Help us see and find the truth and comfort Alexis while—"

"In Jesus's name, Amen." She finished for him before he could pray any more. She opened her eyes. "I love that you prayed, but if I think any more about Theresa—" Her voice broke.

He rubbed the outside of her arms as if she was cold. "You're trying to keep it together," he said softly. "I understand."

Raven pressed her warm torso against the back of Alexis's legs. She reached down to pat the dog's head. "I think she's having a hard time keeping it together, too."

Nick released Alexis. "Are you up for calling the chief again, or would you like me to? He needs to know about the mayor."

"No, I know him. I will. His reaction when I tell him about Gerald will help me figure out the next step."

"Us." He winked. "Help *us* figure out the next step."

He said it so softly she almost missed the inflection. She'd been so used to navigating life and her problems alone lately that she had a hard time accepting that someone else was in this with her. She didn't know what to say, so she merely nodded and picked up the phone.

The chief answered on the third ring. "You'd better be calling to tell me you are on the way over to my station."

She cringed. Chief had been a presence in her life since she was a little girl, when her dad had been the mayor. It went against every fiber of her being to disappoint him, but she didn't see any way around it. "You need to bring Gerald in for questioning," she said. "He's connected to everything. Theresa was his girlfriend—"

"You know, I've had a pretty crummy weekend thus far," Chief interrupted. "Have you still got that dog with you?" Chief's voice crackled with such emotion it caught her off guard.

"Yes," she said tentatively.

"Well, I hope you're taking good care of her." He cleared his throat. "Joe passed away. So we need to figure out who he willed the dog to."

She sat herself down on the metal stool next to the countertop. The dog's owner had passed away? Raven looked up at her as if she didn't have a care in the world. Tears pricked Alexis's eyes. "I thought he was stable."

"He was until someone gave him some of that blasted elephant tranquilizer."

She gasped. What would be the motive for killing Joe? Had it come from the same bottle that had been planted in Nick's hotel room? If she asked, the chief would just tell her to come in again.

Joe had been at the hospital in Boise. Her eyes met Nick's as she tried to piece things together. The back of her mind nagged for attention. Her head hurt from concentrating so hard until it clicked. "The mayor. Theresa said she went out of town with the mayor."

"I've already got Gerald here, Alexis. He practically climbed into a cruiser of his own accord when we were busy trying to get the gunmen rounded up."

"Did you?"

He grunted. "Most of them, but not all. And none of them are talking, so why don't you come in before you get yourselves killed? We can keep you safe here and you can answer a few questions."

"What did Gerald say?" she pressed. "Did he admit to killing Theresa?"

He sighed. "I don't have to tell you a thing, Lexi."

"Chief, you've known me since forever. It's why you can't seem to get my name right." She couldn't resist the dig. "I want justice as much as you do, but I think I have a better chance of getting that outside your station."

He let out a grumble. "Gerald's not talking. He's waiting for his lawyer. The only thing I have to hold him on is a charge of trespassing. I've got a whole lot more that I can charge you with, if we're being honest. So do me a favor and make it easier on the both of us. Come in, and let's figure this out together."

Maybe he was right, and it was time to give up the fight. "Will I be behind bars when we do this figuring?"

Silence answered for a moment before he sighed. "We have witnesses, Alexis."

Cold seeped into her veins. "Wh-what do you mean?"

"Someone in housekeeping at the hotel reported seeing you with the drugs. And management confirmed you left the hotel and returned within an hour in the middle of the night."

"But we didn't!" His words implied more than simple drug possession.

Nick's head and shoulders dropped as he overheard.

"I want to believe you," the chief said, "but the longer you avoid coming in, the worse it looks."

"What about the security camera at the medical clinic?" There had to be something there.

"Nothing. We can't see the door to the employment agency, only the parking lot behind the clinic. Not so much as a stray cat showed up on the footage."

Her heart plummeted. She'd known it was a possibility that the camera wouldn't show the area all the way down to the employment agency, but she'd thought for sure it'd at least show a vehicle driving past. "Do you have a warrant out for me, Chief?"

His two seconds of silence were all the encouragement she needed. He hadn't issued a warrant for their arrest.

"I'm tempted to call your parents," he said, as if she were a teenager instead of a grown woman.

"You go ahead and do that, then." Sarcasm dripped over her words. "You know they'll rush back up here, and it'll be on your head that they'll be put in unnecessary danger." She sighed, knowing she was pushing the boundaries of respectful disagreement. Her parents and the chief were still close friends so she could understand his inclination, but he had to know it would be far worse for them to be there. What if the drug runners put a hit out on them? "I'll think about what you've said and be in touch." She ended the call and stared at her phone as if the solution rested there.

It would be so nice to erase the log of recent calls and pretend it removed the entire day's events, like nothing ever happened.

"I don't have any idea of what we can do next," she said. "If they can't make Gerald talk, then where does that leave us? They have fake witnesses against us, Nick. I don't know how we can win." Her voice rose in pitch despite her effort to remain calm.

The only reason the chief hesitated on the warrant was probably that he didn't want to bother a judge on a holiday weekend, especially because deep down the chief had to know they were innocent. At least, that was her hope. Her hands shook as she dropped her head into them. "We have no proof."

Nick sucked in a sharp breath and tapped the table. "Something's been bothering me. If you're right, and Gerald was the one who killed Joe and broke the glass to kill Theresa, then why wouldn't she tell you that on the message? If I suspected that my mystery girlfriend killed someone and was about to kill me, I would stop keeping secrets. It'd be the first thing on my message. But instead…"

She lifted her head. "It's as if she was still trying to protect him. Or she was hoping that if she kept his secret, then maybe he wouldn't kill her." She swiped on her phone until she came to voice mail and steeled herself to listen to Theresa's message again.

*"We need to talk immediately. In person. I got your message. I think you might be in danger, honey. Where are my stupid time cards?"*

Nick stood and put his hand on her shoulder before she even realized her eyes were filling with tears. It seemed so ironic that Theresa thought Alexis was in danger when in reality her murderer was a mere step away. She blinked back the tears. "You were right. She didn't mention him at all. Odd, but maybe she loved him so much she didn't want to face it."

"Possible," he answered slowly. "But it's worth thinking about other possibilities. What about the time cards? Doesn't it seem odd that it was so important for her to find the time cards in the middle of the night?"

Alexis stared at him without really seeing him. The phone call had come in the middle of the night, which was why she'd missed it in the first place. Theresa wasn't the most organized person on the planet, but she always got the job done.

None of the small business owners Alexis worked for had ever bad-mouthed Theresa. Her employees had a high turnover rate, but that was to be expected at a temp agency. Most employees came and went without much notice, except Deborah, who was a sixty-five-year-old retired teacher. She just did odd jobs to stay busy.

Alexis actually had taken most of the work for the past six months. After two weeks of crying and moping, her mother had told her she had to go do something for someone else for her mental health. So Alexis had volunteered at the food bank, where she'd met Theresa, who had asked what she was doing with her time while she was in town. And before she knew it, Alexis had her very own rut that she was stuck in. But the worry about the time cards didn't make sense.

"I don't know why they would matter so much," she admitted. "But I know somewhere we can find copies."

He exhaled. "Is it going to involve sneaking around town and ending up surrounded by gunmen again?"

As much as she hated to admit it, she needed him. "If I agree that's a possibility, will I be on my own?"

He handed Raven an apple he'd found in a basket on the counter. The dog seemed to inhale it within three crunches. "Come on, girl," he said as his way of answering. "You're the only one of us trained to track secrets and face danger."

# TEN

The temperature of the night air had dropped by several degrees. A chill settled through the flannel shirt Nick wore. He tried to stop the repeated loop playing in his mind: *You're a wanted man.*

He'd done everything by the book to become a respected, valuable member of the community, and for what? If any of this made the news in Seattle, or worse, if he had to call Mom from jail, she would no doubt suffer a heart attack like she had the night his brother passed away. He didn't know if her heart could handle another shock.

He held the leash, but Raven ran ahead and heeled at Alexis's feet instead of his own. He didn't bother correcting the action, though he tried to tell himself it wasn't because he was hoping Alexis would grow to be a dog person.

Alexis opened the side gate and led them to the closest sidewalk. "People might start to come home from the celebration soon, so it shouldn't look too odd to see a couple out for a walk with our dog."

He liked the sound of a moonlit stroll as a couple with *their* dog. "There's just one problem. Most everyone in town seems to know who you are."

She pointed at a sign in the front yard that said Vote Kendrick for Mayor. "I don't think I'm the only one with that problem."

If they hadn't been on the run, he would have taken it as a compliment. He loved the idea that the town might embrace him. "So, we just keep our heads down when a car passes."

"Wrong. That's big city thinking. Small-town residents always take a moment to look and see if they know the person on the side of the road." She shrugged. "Then they roll down the window and say hello."

He grinned at the thought. "I guess I haven't been living the small-town way. If we ever get out of this, that sounds nice."

She asked him to stay put for a second as she returned the house key underneath the doormat where she'd found it. She pointed to the left. "Let's turn here. This street doesn't get as much traffic. If we stay behind the tree line, we should be able to get back to my house without being spotted. If you see a car, though—"

"Make like a tree and leave?"

She glared at him, but her lips fought and lost. A laugh escaped and she rolled her eyes. "Well, you got the 'make like a tree' part right."

They were going back to her house. He assumed that meant her parents' house. "Why are we going to your place? Do you have the time cards?"

She tilted her hand at diagonal angles as if debating it in her head before answering. "Yes and no. All the temp agency time cards were hard copies."

"As in pen and paper? That's rare in this day and age."

"Exactly. I thought it was odd, too, but Theresa said that a lot of her clients preferred it that way. To be fair, many of the small business owners are getting up there in age and haven't quite embraced technology. At least, that was her explanation. Now, I wonder."

"You don't think Theresa was involved in the drug operation?"

Her eyes widened in the moonlight. "No! She told me it was Barry's preference, as well—he took care of all the bookkeeping and payroll. He said pen and paper couldn't be hacked."

"Barry is the mayor's brother. The one with the investment firm?"

She nodded. "And the reason Gerald struck it big on the stock market. Seems like everyone invested with him after that. Did you?"

Nick had been tempted. Barry came highly recommended, but when Nick had gone in to discuss it, he came away concerned with Barry's antiquated system. After some research, he decided he could manage his practice's finances himself with the help of some expensive software. He might feel different after rebuilding the practice. His fingers itched to call his insurance company, even if they were closed over the holiday weekend.

"So the only reason people invested was that Gerald had some impressive dividends?"

She frowned. "No. Other older folks made out pretty well." She pursed her lips. "Given the drug angle, it sounds suspicious, doesn't it? I worked for him, temped for him and never even blinked an eye."

"So you didn't suspect anything odd, then?"

"No, but I mainly filed paperwork, entered numbers in spreadsheets—"

"So he wasn't totally computer illiterate." He shrugged. "It's worth exploring, at least. Did you invest with him?"

She pressed her lips together. "I have no money to invest."

"Your parents, then?"

"They wanted to, so I wouldn't be surprised."

"How do the time cards work into his paper and pen methods?"

"He puts them in the shredder after he enters them into the software."

Nick frowned. "That doesn't jibe with the 'this way we won't get hacked' mentality. So you have some that aren't shredded?"

"I'm too type A just to hand over the hard copies without digital accountability."

"No," he said with an exaggerated tone and a wink. "You? Type A?"

She smacked him playfully on the arm. He faked injury, but she ignored him and continued. "So I took photographs of each time card with my smartphone before I submitted it to Theresa."

"Was your pay ever inconsistent?"

She shook her head. "No, I never had a problem."

"But the photos are no longer on your phone." He held up a hand. "Let me guess. You import them onto a backup drive every six weeks."

She bristled. "Every week, if you must know, and it's not a backup drive. It's a laptop." She sighed. "I want to have hope that there's a clue there, but you know in all likelihood, it's going to be nothing."

While true, he preferred hanging onto hope rather than the alternative. The pressure from the day and the seriousness of the matter threatened to overwhelm him, as if it hovered on the back of his neck, ready to paralyze him. He needed to capture his thoughts, or at least avoid thinking about them for a while, or he might self-destruct.

Car beams swung around the corner a block ahead. He took a step backward into the shadows and tugged gently on Alexis's elbow to get her to follow him. As soon as Raven saw they were still, she flopped down on the ground like she wanted to take a nap right there. The poor dog was overdue for a nice, long snooze.

The car blared rock music, but they remained silent. How many squirrels and birds made the wide branches above them their home? He could hardly make out any moonlight when he looked straight up. The tree at their backs had to be one of the widest cedars he'd ever seen. His gaze dropped to find Alexis staring at him curiously.

Heat filled his chest. He couldn't look away. "You're beautiful." The words came out in a whisper, so fast he couldn't stop them.

She blinked, and the moment of connection dissipated into the night.

He wanted to kick himself. What was he doing? She'd made it abundantly clear that she had no plans to date anyone in town. She wouldn't be sticking around. He didn't need a surefire recipe to heartache. And yet he found himself growing increasingly attracted to her.

Alexis grew prettier the more he got to know her. The opposite usually happened as he got to know women. He didn't know what to make of it.

She scoffed, "Everyone looks good in moonlight."

First of all, that wasn't true, but if she thought it was… "Are you're saying I look good?" he asked.

She pressed her lips to one side and rolled her eyes.

"If you're not, I think I've just proved your theory has holes." He couldn't help but flash his best smile.

She put her head down, but not before he could see the smile forming. "Car's gone," she said and strode ahead of him down the street. Raven rushed after her, almost dragging him by the leash. *Who's walking who?*

Alexis looked over her shoulder. "One more block, and then I know a shortcut through a field where we should be safe from prying eyes."

He picked up his pace to match hers. The playful moment had disappeared, and with the reminder that they weren't safe, the heaviness that had hung over him returned. It warred with the peace that at moments calmed his heart. The war of emotions left him exhausted. The grass up ahead looked good enough to sleep on.

She turned left onto a dirt path marred by weeds and grass. The trees around the abandoned field blocked the streetlights in the distance. Only the moon and the stars lit their way.

With concern, he watched Raven walk. "I'll look at her paws the moment we have light. We'll need to check her for stickers."

"You mean goat heads."

Within the first week of moving to the county, he'd

tried to take his bike onto the rural roads. People had warned him about goat heads. He'd imagined the road must be littered with goat skeletons and wondered what kind of odd place he'd moved to, until the stickers had punctured his bike wheels and he'd realized they looked like goat heads.

Alexis looked down at Raven. "I'll try to keep an eye on her and make sure she doesn't start limping," she whispered. "You always wanted to be a veterinarian?"

"Um. No. I started in premed, but I could see the writing on the wall my senior year, so I took an animal biology class just in case. Didn't stop me from my path to medical school, though. Didn't even last a semester before I knew I needed to transfer to a vet school."

"You wanted to be a doctor?" Her tone had a measure of disbelief.

"I always knew I wanted to help people, but it became clear I wouldn't be able to handle it."

She tilted her head. "Why? The blood?" She shivered. "Sorry. Obviously, there's blood involved in being a vet. I wouldn't be able to do it. I can't even stand to think about it."

"No." He still remembered getting the news that his grandfather had passed away from lung cancer. His death had been the final straw for Nick. And everyone at the university had figured out he was done before he had. His cheeks heated at the memories. "I couldn't cope when patients made bad choices to the detriment of their health. I couldn't control people."

"I can understand that," she said softly.

"The clients who bring their animals in to me are,

ninety-nine percent of the time, good owners who will do almost anything to make sure their pets stay well."

"Don't you have to deal with bad owners sometimes?"

"There are laws on my side in that event. There aren't any laws that say people have to stop smoking after they've been diagnosed with lung cancer."

Raven lifted her nose and nuzzled his hand. He pushed the painful memories into the back of his mind. "And animals are easy to love and forgive. It seemed like an easy choice to go into veterinary medicine." He lifted his gaze. They were coming to the edge of the clearing. Now that they were visible through the thin line of trees, they would have to be on guard again. He sighed. "I would ask you why you became a lawyer, but—"

Her entire body stiffened, and her stride grew longer. "You've figured out that's a topic I don't like to talk about."

He nodded but let her words hang in the air.

She eyed him right before she stepped in between the trees. "You do look good in the moonlight, by the way."

He stumbled over a tree root as he processed her words. She must have finally decided she didn't want him poking holes in the theory of hers that said everyone looked good in the moonlight.

He caught up to her as she moved onto the sidewalk, but before he could respond with a flirtatious quip, the surroundings took him by surprise. A block away, a hollowed-out shell of a building with a caved-in roof stood as a reminder that, if they couldn't prove their innocence, his entire life would crumble.

"Nick," Alexis whispered. "The silver car that was at the corner before the fire is back on my street."

Alexis stood paralyzed at the tree line. Her insides shook just seeing the car. True, they had no proof it was associated with the fire, but the least the police could do would be to ask the owner of it a few questions. It had to be the same car, but when she called, she would reveal her and Nick's whereabouts. She needed to be sure it was worth the risk.

Nick pulled her back into the shadows. "Call the police."

"You're sure it's the right move?" Alexis envied the certainty in his voice. She used to make quick decisions with confidence. She fumbled to get her phone.

"No, I'm not, but I think at this point, we'd better be safe than sorry."

Alexis stared at him. She wanted to hear him say that if they called the police, everything was going to be all right. Because people who did the right things were supposed to end up having a good life, not to get hauled off to prison for something they didn't do.

It was the very reason she'd never wanted to be a defense lawyer. Somewhere deep inside, she assumed that all accused people were likely guilty or they wouldn't have been accused in the first place. If this was to be the year in which God put a spotlight on every corner of her heart to reveal all her prejudices and misguided notions, she prayed He would just write her a detailed letter instead. The Bible instantly came to mind.

She hesitated to dial the emergency line. After her last conversation, she didn't want to call the chief, either. Jeremy's contact information was at the top of her list. The phone rang two times before he answered. "Jeremy, the silv—"

"Stop calling me," he interrupted. "I mean it. Unless you're ready to have me pick you up or come in of your own accord, I'm not helping you."

"But—"

"You of all people should know that I can't make concessions for friends. The law is the law. Don't put me in this position again." A dial tone sounded in her ear.

"Sounds like that went well," Nick said drily. "Maybe we should take a peek before we call again. It's possible it's someone visiting one of these houses, right?"

"Not very." They would've parked closer or in the driveway if that were the case.

They stuck to the shadows as they crossed the street and neared the vehicle. Over her shoulder, her parents' house beckoned her. The fridge was full of leftovers and cold iced tea and—

A flick of light through the bay window made her breath catch. But it was only for a second. She blinked to make sure her eyes hadn't played a trick on her. She turned around, searching for another source of light. "Nick, did you see—"

Raven barked at the driver's side door of the silver car.

"Shh," Alexis and Nick both hissed at the dog at the same time.

Raven responded by nudging her nose at the bottom of the door and barking again. She sat down, wagging her tail.

Alexis tugged on Nick's elbow as they ran around the end of the car. "Get down," she whispered. "I saw a light inside my house."

Nick groaned. "Call the police now. If they find someone in the house, that'll give them probable cause to search this car. And Raven seems very sure something is in this vehicle."

Alexis dialed 911. "There's a burglary in progress at 1415 Jefferson." She hung up before the dispatcher could ask any more questions. Light reflected on the street underneath the car. "Why can't they train the dog to sniff loudly instead of bark?"

"Let's just pray that the burglar doesn't have a gun."

The light disappeared as fast as it appeared. Nick straightened painfully slowly until he peeked through the windows of the car. "I don't see anyone approaching."

Her heart sped up. "What if he's getting away? He's probably Theresa's murderer."

Nick's eyes widened. "Why would someone be searching your house?"

Her throat seemed to close. She choked out, "To kill me."

Nick blinked, unfazed. "Or?"

"The time cards?"

He nodded. "I like that option better, but how would they know you have some? Did Theresa know you took pictures of the time cards before you turned them in?"

Alexis racked her brain. "One time I forgot to take a snapshot until I reached her office to turn them in. She witnessed me taking the photos. So, yes. She didn't mind. She teased me about it, in fact. It's…it's possible she told Gerald or someone that I kept digital copies. Maybe that's why she was frantically searching for her copies."

"So if our theory is correct, then your nighttime visitor might be after the cards. Theresa said you were probably in danger. It's possible she knew. Maybe that's why she was frantically trying to find her copies of the time cards."

She nodded toward the house. "Well, if that's what he's after, he won't find them in there."

"He won't?"

"No." She chanced a look through the car windows to catch a view across the street. "Most people assume I live in the house. I don't. I have an apartment above the garage."

A beam of light illuminated the kitchen for a brief moment, enough to see a dark figure lurking about the house. "I don't think he saw us," Nick said. "He must have thought a dog in the neighborhood was barking."

The police were on their way. Alexis hoped the cops had sense enough to keep the sirens off when they approached. The light beam went off again.

"Can you see the house from your apartment?"

She nodded. "Let's go get the time cards. If the cops don't get here in time, we can watch and see where he goes." Nick crossed the street with Raven at his heels before she could object.

She rushed after him. "What if he has a gun?"

Nick's steps faltered. "I wasn't going to confront him. I'm hoping he doesn't see us at all."

"I like that plan." Her heart raced faster the closer they got to her parents' house. They crouched in front of the bushes as they slipped past the bay window. While it served her purposes not to have motion-detecting lights at the moment, if she got out of this alive, she would install some herself. Maybe that would've been enough to deter the intruder. Though if he'd murdered Theresa, she doubted it. A chill ran down her spine at the thought.

Nick led the way, but she realized he didn't know where he was going. She tapped his shoulder, and he let her pass him and Raven. Once she rounded the corner, she'd be at the house threshold. The entrance to the garage was almost directly across from the front door. The space in between acted almost like an outdoor hallway.

She held a hand up to Nick to indicate he should stay put and keep a look out while she opened the side door to the garage. Her eyes strained to see more as she watched the front door before she stepped up to the entrance to her garage apartment. She slipped her apartment key from her jeans and inserted it into the lock.

A steel arm wrapped around her neck, closing off the oxygen. She shoved her elbow backward. Her attacker shifted and her arm thrashed into thin air. He pressed harder into her esophagus. Something sharp dug into her right side. She couldn't think straight enough to decipher if it was a gun or not.

A deep voice rasped into her ear. "Where are the time cards?" Something sounded familiar about it, but the panic and lack of oxygen made her thoughts muddy.

His arm went slack as shards of ceramic rained over her shoulder, stinging but welcome compared to the vise around her neck. She sucked in a deep breath. The attacker fell to the ground. Soil and wilted geraniums littered around his face, which was covered by a ski mask.

Nick's hands dropped from the air.

Alexis cradled her neck with her fingers, desperate to ease the tight pain in her throat. "Gun." She could barely get the word out as a croak. Raven barked at the man but didn't move to attack.

Nick stomped on the man's right forearm, so he must have heard Alexis over Raven's bark. The man howled and released the gun. Nick kicked it aside, but the attacker took that moment to swipe at his other leg, and Nick fell back. Alexis lunged and braced Nick with her outstretched arm.

He regained his balance, but when they both turned, the man had disappeared. Nick grabbed her arm and shoved her toward the door. "He might've found the—"

A bullet shot into the night before he could finish his thought. It whizzed past them and found its mark in the headlight of a police cruiser pulling up to the scene. Nick shoved her inside the apartment entrance and closed the door behind her. "Let's hope they realize we weren't the ones who shot at them."

She held on to the possibility that the officers hadn't even seen them since they were in the shadows, but her throat hurt too much to voice it. Sirens sounded in the street. The police weren't keeping their presence on the down low now after being shot at.

"Keep a watch out, I'll be right back." Alexis ran up the steps inside the garage to her apartment. She flung open the door and flipped on her smartphone's flashlight function. There were only two small windows in the back of the apartment, both facing the back-yard, but they were covered with blinds and curtains.

From the street, the building likely looked like a tall garage for an RV. That was, after all, its function before her parents had renovated it into an apartment, intending it at one time to be a possible income source. They had no idea that their only daughter, a lawyer, would end up moving back home to lick her wounds.

The furniture fit in the one-bedroom, one-bathroom studio like a game of Tetris. Her desk sat between the table and the bed. She launched across the strip of tile and shoved the laptop into the computer bag. At least she knew someone wanted those time cards, so they had to be on to something. If she could just get a mo-ment of peace and quiet, maybe she would figure out the motive behind Theresa's murder and have proof of their innocence.

She felt before she saw a figure looming in the doorway. Her muscles tensed. Her fingers reached for a glass paperweight as the only weapon she could find. Her beam of light focused on Nick and her shoul-ders dropped. He was supposed to have stayed put. Her poor heart couldn't handle another scare, and her throat still wasn't ready for her to try talking.

"Please," Nick said, "tell me you still have your parents' car keys."

She nodded and reached for them. Though she couldn't imagine what good they would do when her dad's car was likely still near Theresa's house, or worse, impounded.

Nick rushed toward her and took them from her hand, studying them in the glow of her phone. A grin crossed his face. "The police are searching next door. It'll take them only a few minutes to realize someone is in here. Can we go?"

She nodded and pulled the strap of the laptop bag across her torso. An open water bottle sat on the edge of the desk. She greedily gulped it as she ran after Nick, back down the stairs. The liquid instantly helped ease some of the soreness. "Where's Raven?" Her voice sounded stronger but still hoarse.

"You'll see. Turn off the phone light before the cops notice."

"Those two sentences contradict each other," she whispered. She grabbed his shoulder in front of her as she turned the beam off and descended the stairs. She hadn't been counting the steps and wouldn't know when they'd come to the bottom. As she fell into the space between his shoulder blades, she knew they'd reached the ground.

"Stay here a second." The sound of metal and greasy wheels echoed through the garage. Light from the moon streamed into the back. Nick stood underneath the open garage door that led into the backyard. When her dad had renovated, he'd made it into a drive-through garage so he could easily take his riding lawnmower out in the backyard. Seemed like overkill given they had only a third of an acre, but it'd made her dad happy.

Raven sat in the sidecar of the old Honda cruiser motorcycle. Nick held something in his hands. "Think fast." What looked like a dark ball volleyed into the air. She barely caught it with her fingertips and felt the opening to the helmet.

"Seriously?" she whispered despite the pain.

He threw his hands up at the otherwise empty garage. "Do you have a better idea?"

If she had, she would've argued, but the angry voices of officers yelling spurred her forward. A gunshot rang out but seemed farther away. The burglar was still out there?

Nick straddled the motorcycle and gestured for her to hop on behind him. She slapped on the helmet and adjusted the laptop bag to lie flat against her back. A harness of sorts, made from the pink leash, crisscrossed around the dog's torso and attached to the seat belt Alexis's dad had installed in the sidecar. Instead of a helmet, Raven wore her mom's old white driving goggles.

"Let's hope this starts." Nick slipped the key into the ignition and cranked the handles. It sputtered before it revved to life.

"Go left." She pointed with her left hand over his shoulder before the cruiser lurched forward. Without a backrest, wrapping her arms around his torso couldn't be avoided. She tried not to notice how surprisingly solid the veterinarian was and instead focused on a decision that she would start a jogging routine if they survived.

The bike and sidecar spun into the yard and shot across diagonally to the alley. Except the sidecar lifted off the ground as Nick made the turn. Alexis held in her instinct to scream and fought against the momentum by leaning hard right. Raven licked her arm as she did so, which almost made Alexis let go of her hold on Nick's torso.

He straightened the bike, and Raven's seat settled back on the ground.

Over her shoulder, flashlights darted inside her parents' house, but no beams were directed at them. Surely they had heard the engine, but maybe they assumed it was someone on the street. Though if they had gotten away without being spotted, what about the burglar?

Another gunshot rang out, and gravel sprayed to her right. A police officer wouldn't have shot without at least calling for them to stop. She was sure of it. The silver vehicle sped out from the side street, windows down, lights off. The motorcycle beam caught the man's eyes as he leaned out of the passenger window, but the ski mask still covered the rest of his face.

She squeezed Nick tighter at the memory of what the burglar's arm felt like around her throat. If not for the helmet, she would've buried her face in his shirt until it was all over.

"Turn right," she yelled. The strain hurt, but it was the only way to be heard. Nick rotated the handlebars and turned into what looked like a long driveway, but Alexis knew better. The small town had more alleys than streets, but the property owners were responsible for maintaining them. The three property owners of this little stretch were the only ones to contribute the money to pave it.

Nick narrowly avoided a trash can. Lights flashed on in different houses. Sirens grew closer. Raven's nose worked overtime in the air as if she didn't have a care in the world.

The silver car revved behind them and another gunshot sounded, this time spinning the trash can into the alley. The burglar had made it to his getaway car but chose to pursue them rather than escape from the police. Why? Her gut churned as she recalled the feeling of cold metal pressed into her side. If it were more important for him to kill them than to avoid getting caught by the police, how would they ever survive?

# ELEVEN

Of all the bad ideas Nick had ever had in his life, this by far was his worst. He hadn't ridden a motorcycle since his late teens, and driving with a sidecar proved to be a completely different beast. On a regular bike, he had to compensate with each turn, but with the sidecar, he had to brake and throttle less to turn left and add throttle to make a right turn. The wheels felt squishy and insecure on the gravel, and the trigger-happy driver behind them was enough to make his head explode with stress.

He took the next street without Alexis's guidance, and it ended up being a long driveway. He revved the throttle, jumped the curb and drove diagonally across the front lawn until he came to the next driveway and took the very next right turn. The gunshots stopped momentarily, but he kept his speed as high as possible.

Two turns later, Alexis patted his shoulder. "You lost them. At least for a moment."

His breathing and heart rate weren't sure they should believe her quite yet, but there were no longer headlights in the side mirrors. The library on his right caught his attention. He swung into the parking lot and slipped behind the building into a spot where the overhead lights didn't reach them. He flicked off the ignition, and everything went dark and quiet.

They both breathed heavier than normal. Raven panted happily but stayed still in the sidecar.

"I'll tell you one thing," he whispered. "If somehow I still become mayor, my first act will be paving all those alleys."

Alexis dropped her helmet-covered head between his shoulder blades and exhaled. He'd have objected to the discomfort, but she was either crying or exhausted, so he remained motionless, his hands still on the handlebars.

Raven looked expectantly at him. Nick removed the goggles. He had no intention of driving the motorcycle even two more feet unless they were held at gunpoint again. He scratched behind Raven's ear. "Who's a good dog?"

She panted like she already knew she was a rock star.

The weight lifted from his back. "Yes, you are," Alexis cooed in hushed tones. She reached over and scratched the dog behind the ears, too, something Nick had thought he'd never see. Raven looked so happy, practically smiling as her mouth hung open. If she hadn't been wearing the homemade harness, Nick felt certain Raven would've ended up in Alexis's lap.

The rev of an engine and sirens approached at high speed. Alexis placed one arm around his waist as if they were about to take off again. The warmth from her embrace made his thoughts muddy, though he told himself it was probably more from exhaustion and lack of food.

The passing lights illuminated a newspaper box on the corner of the sidewalk, next to the back library entrance. He blinked but felt certain his and Alexis's faces were plastered on the front page of *The Barings Herald.* He slipped off the motorcycle and rolled it, passengers and all, until it was deeper in the shadows.

Alexis slipped off her helmet and wordlessly helped him untangle the leash knots and remove it from the seat belt. The farther away the sirens became, the more he could relax.

"I hope they catch the burglar," she whispered.

He walked to the newspaper box without her, clicked on his phone and held it close enough to the box that it wouldn't reflect into the night.

The headline read Mayoral Candidate and Disbarred Attorney Accused of Ties to Drug Ring.

He squinted at the first line of the article. "According to an anonymous source, drugs were found—"

Alexis gasped behind him. She fumbled in her pocket, reached around him and placed a few quarters in the slot, then pulled out the paper. Nick straightened. So he finally knew why she didn't practice law, but unfortunately, so did the rest of the town. Judging by her heartbroken expression, this would be news to everyone.

Her own phone illuminated the front page. The second half of the article included a photograph of Alexis and Nick in the back of a squad car. He groaned. That looked bad. The final photograph, while blurrier, showed Alexis and Nick clasping hands on the cliff. It had been right after she'd helped him to standing, but more importantly, who took the photograph?

The angle looked to be from above. "Who's the photographer?"

Her wide eyes met his. "I'm so sorry, Nick. I didn't want to damage your campaign."

"My campaign was probably over the moment someone planted drugs in my room. I'm just sorry the media pulled you into this."

She shook her head. "You're not going to ask me if I really did it?"

"Did what? Let an alleged murderer go free?"

"They're twisting it. I broke privilege." Her head hung. "But it resulted in a murderer walking free."

"I figured it had to be something like that since you stopped practicing law. But look at the photo—"

Her jaw and arm dropped, taking the paper with it, as she shook her head. "And that doesn't bother you?"

"Well, I don't know all the details. Would you rather I be upset?" An exasperated sigh escaped before he could contain it. "Look, I'm sure there's a story behind it, but I really want to know who took that photograph of us on the cliff."

"It said anonymous."

"Can they do that? Don't they need our permission to—"

Her eyes flashed with fiery heat. "The photographer didn't need our consent as we were in a public place. You know I wasn't a defense attorney, right? I was disbarred." She barely took a breath. "Still don't care? 'Cause if you really don't, then I'm happy to be your campaign manager." Her voice rose as her words tripped over each other. She threw her hands in front of her, one hand waving the paper. She may have been talking about his campaign, but her tone and the look in her eyes seemed to be saying more. "They may have twisted the facts, but the result is still the same. I'm responsible for a murderer walking the streets of Seattle. The truth is, it'll destroy your reputation because everyone else in this town will care. They'll care a lot."

Nick stared at her as he tried to process her words. "Like I said, I'm pretty sure people will care more about our suspected association to a drug ring. The word is out. We're running out of time to clear our names."

Raven whimpered and pressed herself into the side of Alexis's leg. She slumped. "Sorry," she whispered. "Everything's out of control, and I just took it out on you. I have no excuse."

Even in the moonlight, he could see the fiery shade of red blossom over her neck and cheeks. She dipped her chin. "I've been ashamed so long. To see it in print…"

He lifted the paper from her fingertips. "Maybe I'm more tired than I want to admit, but I find it hard to believe that the woman in front of me who dreams of advocating for the elderly, who babysat and served her community in word and deed her entire childhood, would intentionally let a murderer go. And until you tell me your side—or let me read this article—I refuse to think anything but the best of you."

She took a step closer to him, her eyes cross-examining his features. His heart raced at her closeness. It was pointless to deny he was falling for her hard despite his best intentions.

"Innocent until proven guilty?" she asked.

"Shouldn't it be that way? I certainly wish someone would give me that benefit of the doubt."

She reached out with her right hand and rested it on his shoulder. He glanced at her fingertips and felt her lips brush his cheek. He closed his eyes and struggled not to pull her into his arms. He turned toward her, but she didn't move away.

His left hand slid across her neck and into her silky hair. He bent his head and leaned forward to—

Raven shoved herself between their legs. Alexis blinked as if waking up from a dream and stared at the dog. A soft smile crossed her face.

Never before had he disliked a dog as much as he did at the moment. Although, maybe Raven was trying to protect them both from broken hearts. "I... I guess we should go before they retrace their steps. It won't take them long to find us."

She walked toward the motorcycle.

He shook his head. "I think there's nothing more noticeable than a dog in a sidecar. Did your dad have to go through additional training before driving your mom in that?" He gestured at the scrapes on the side of the sidecar. "It was harder to handle than I thought."

She shrugged. She'd never taken any interest in learning how to drive it. "Actually, it was my mom's motorcycle. Dad wanted to have her drive him around in the town parades so he could wave like those men in the little cars, with the additional benefit of getting to throw candy."

"Like the Shriners?" He laughed. "I wish I could've seen that. Your parents sound like fun people."

They were fun people until she had come home in

a depressed funk. She hoped Arizona was treating them right. "You would like them. Dad made a good mayor." She pointed to the line of trees bordering the back of the parking lot. "We'd better move quickly. It's a good five-minute walk back to Joe's."

He cringed.

"I know," she said before he could comment. "It feels wrong to stay at a dead man's house, but he would want Raven to eat, rest and be comfortable. It'll give us a chance to look at the time cards and re-group." She put a hand between the laptop bag strap and her neck with a grimace. Her spine and muscles might never be the same after the past few days.

Nick slipped a finger underneath the strap on her shoulder. She faltered as he wordlessly lifted the bag off her and placed it on his shoulder. How she wanted to kiss him. It probably had been for the best that Raven had interfered. It would've just complicated everything even more. If they ever got out of this, her situation remained the same. There was no reason to stay in Barings. Once her parents' house sold, she'd have nowhere to stay and no job. Falling for him had to remain off the table. Even though he woke up her mind and her heart in a way no one else ever had. He'd proved himself to be trustworthy and a good man.

"I wanted to tell you," she said softly as they walked in the shadows. "Before the story came out. I wanted you to know."

"So tell me now. Unless you'd rather I read about it."

She took a deep breath and focused on the path ahead. "I haven't told anyone but my parents. I've been writing small web articles for different content farms for pennies just so it'd drive the article down in the search rankings. It'd take a while to sort through all the Alexis Thompson hits—it's not a rare name—but you could find it on the internet. Eventually."

"So it's been in the news before?"

She nodded. "I was a patent lawyer, and my client was in a David-and-Goliath-type case." Her lips lifted in a sad smile. "I was going to win. Out of the blue, he told me he had killed his partner. He had faked evidence that made everyone believe his partner had just left the country. He told me every detail." Her stride diminished, and her steps faltered as she recalled everything. "So, after countless sleepless nights, I called in an anonymous tip. Only it eventually came to light that I was the informant."

"Does it really fall under attorney-client privilege when you weren't his defense lawyer?"

"Unfortunately." She sucked in a breath. "But I argued it was the exception to 'prevent, mitigate or rectify substantial injury to the financial interests of another that is reasonably certain to result or has resulted from the client's commission of a crime in furtherance of which the client has used the lawyer's services.'" She huffed. "Can you tell I memorized the rules from the American Bar Association? Basically I argued that if I helped my client in the patent case, he had a good chance of winning substantial money that his partner's family would never receive. Not to mention the wife couldn't get life insurance because everyone thought he'd left her. I felt part of the crime. I couldn't work, I couldn't eat…" Her throat and nose burned with held-back tears.

"You had no idea that would happen. You were a patent lawyer."

His gentle voice and understanding nature weren't helping her keep it together. She refused to let her guard down, so she pulled back her shoulders. "No. But when I entered this profession, I should've been willing to live with the consequences if it did happen. In the state of Washington, at least, they ruled I should've kept my mouth shut. I was disbarred. All of my lawyer friends agreed with the verdict, and worse, the murderer got to walk free. That poor family knows that he did it, and yet he walks free."

He reached for her hand and squeezed. "You were just trying to do the right thing."

She sighed and savored the comfort. "You are a good man, Nick. I can't stand the thought of being the reason you can't be mayor, then state senator, then…"

"Not that it matters, but I don't have those kinds of aspirations."

She gently pulled her hand out of his. "That's what my dad said before he became mayor. He soon realized that he could help so many more people if he had a bigger circle of influence. Everyone realized it. He had a huge support group encouraging him to do it."

Nick folded his arms across his chest and tried not to be bothered that she had pulled her hand back. "So, did he run for other offices?"

She shook her head. "I got into the wrong crowd for a brief time in high school, and he didn't want the press to scrutinize my choices. So he put his dreams on hold until recently. And then… Well, you know." She cringed. "I'm thankful and ashamed all at the same time." She shook the paper in her hand. "Obviously he was right to fear the press, but who knows how much good he would've done for the state if it weren't for me?"

"You can't think that way, Alexis. You can't allow past circumstances to dictate your future."

"Why not?" Her voice took on a steely quality. She was so tired of that clichéd sentiment. The past had consequences, plain and simple. "Isn't that why you're running in the first place? Because you want to do the good that your brother would've done had he lived?"

He cringed.

Her gut dropped. Her words had consequences, too. "Oh, Nick. I'm sorry. I shouldn't have said that."

"No, you're right to think that. It's true."

She closed her eyes, unable to handle the pain that crossed his features. "Even if it was true, I shouldn't have said it that way. You were trying to encourage me, and I got defensive."

"No, you spoke the truth. I can't judge you, because I'm guilty of the same thing. The past has called the shots in my decisions lately. The bottom line is, I've lived with the guilt of being the surviving brother every single day, but I want to honor my brother. For him it was much more than a job. He genuinely wanted to help make the world a better place. So if we get our names cleared and the danger disappears, I'll still run for mayor." He exhaled. "Truth is, I'm scared I won't be able to handle it."

"I have no doubt your brother would be so proud." She tilted her head, wondering if she'd missed something. Nick was more than competent and educated. "Why would you think you couldn't handle it?"

"For the same reason that I couldn't handle medical school."

She exhaled, remembering what he'd said. "Because you can't control people." She struggled with that daily, as well. "You can't make them choose the right decisions. I feel the same way, but it doesn't mean you should give up and stop trying."

The words sounded right, but they didn't entirely reflect her heart. She was falling for this man, hard. Deep down, she wished he'd give up the campaign and his practice, and they could move to the city and pursue what seemed to be happening between them. Why did God have to show her this man who seemed perfect for her but then have his life goals revolve around politics and animals? The two things she could never be a part of.

Raven rushed ahead of them and pulled to the left. They had reached Joe's backyard. Alexis unlocked the door. Raven ran through the house, searching for her owner. Tears pricked Alexis's eyes as she watched.

They both stood in the entryway, motionless, until Raven ran back to them.

Alexis leaned down and rubbed her head. "How do you tell a dog its owner is gone?" Her voice cracked.

Nick took a knee. Raven flopped to the ground for him to rub her tummy. "I have no idea."

Alexis walked through the house and made sure all the blinds and curtains were closed before she flipped on the pantry light in the kitchen. It spread at just the right angle that it hit the circular table without filling the room with light. While Joe's passing hadn't made the news yet, she knew it would circulate through the town by the morning.

She spread out the newspaper and stared at the photographs. Her hands shook as she recalled the feeling of almost going over the cliff. For the briefest of moments, she thought she'd been responsible for Nick's death. She cleared her throat to keep it from closing. "Nick, remember when you saw someone on that cliff above us? Maybe when you thought you saw a gun, it was actually a camera. This had to be shot with a telephoto lens."

He joined her at the small table. "Possible. That's why I wanted to know who took the photo."

She pointed to the byline. "I know Tommy from temping at the paper. I'm calling him."

"It's midnight."

"The news never sleeps."

His lips curled into an adorable smile. "I'm pretty sure that's not a thing."

"I'm pretty sure I've heard it somewhere." She dialed and put it on speakerphone.

"Hello?" Tommy answered.

She turned away from Nick's smirk, knowing he could hear how groggy the voice on the other end of the line sounded. She got right to the point. "Tommy, where did you get those photographs of Nick and me?"

"Lexi?" She could hear what sounded like sheets shifting in the background. "I'm sorry. I had to print it. It's news."

The brutal headline would plague her nightmares, but a quick skim of the article showed it focused on the facts alone. She wondered which editor made the call to print it, though. "I'm not blaming you. I want to know where those photographs came from."

"They're anonymous."

"You must have some idea of where they came from."

"Someone used one of those temporary email addresses with a Dropbox invitation. The Dropbox account deleted after I downloaded it."

"And you printed it without a reputable source?"

"It came with links to some Seattle news outlets and the American Bar Association. Those were reputable enough for us to take the lead. If it's any consolation, maybe it's someone who really doesn't want to see Mr. Kendrick get elected. You just happened to be a casualty."

She shivered at the last word. But it was clear that this was another dead end. "Okay, Tommy. Go back to sleep."

"I really am sorry, Lexi. I hope you'll keep filling in for us in ad copy."

It hit her like a brick. She couldn't. Even if there hadn't been drugs and fake witnesses against her or a group of drug traffickers determined to kill her, something inside had shifted.

Her shameful secret had come into the light, and she was ready to face it. If she and Nick were able to walk freely again, she would go after her Idaho license. And even if the bar association said no, she'd do something…anything that challenged her mind and engaged her heart. It'd taken being in danger to realize she'd put her life on hold.

She opened the laptop and clicked on the file where she kept the images of the time cards. Nick placed a plate of sandwiches next to her. "Peanut butter and jelly," he said.

She almost inhaled one. She'd taken three bites

without so much as tasting it. Raven appeared at her side. She tore off an edge and dropped it. "I think the dog approves."

"She certainly approves of you."

"I meant the sandwiches." She eagerly took another bite.

"I know." He leaned over her shoulder and looked at the images. "What are we looking for?"

His proximity made it hard not to focus on the fact they'd almost kissed minutes ago. "Um, I'm not sure. Anything that seems out of place."

"They don't all look the same." He pointed at the screen. "The copy shop ones look different than the newspaper ones. The heating-and-air shop orders the information in a completely different way than the medical practice."

That fact had never bothered her before. They were different companies with different logos. But the form in and of itself should've been in the same order. "Maybe they had to design their own time cards?"

He straightened and put his fists on his waist. "It doesn't add up."

"Well, there has to be something here if someone was willing to kill for them."

"Did Theresa have a scanner?" He pointed to the right side of each image. "These aren't standard time cards. They have what looks like a bar code, except it's half the size of a typical one. And what are all these project numbers?"

She shrugged. "I never asked. I assume it's the account number for Theresa to reference." The familiar ache in between her shoulder blades returned. She recognized it instantly as shame for not being more aware. She'd missed so much during her time of self-centered pity. "I'm afraid I considered it beyond my pay grade and never asked."

"Too bad you weren't a tax attorney."

"Yeah. I've got nothing beyond a rudimentary understanding. But a certified fraud examiner would!" She grabbed her phone and scrolled through her contacts until she found her old college friend, Victoria Hayes. Correction. Victoria Tucker now. Her dear friend had gotten married to a handsome skydiving instructor named Jeff a year ago in Boise. Alexis still wasn't used to calling her by her married name.

She sent the text message and waited.

Victoria was always quick to respond.

"It's one in the morning now, Alexis. Maybe she has her phone set to Do Not Disturb like the rest of us."

Alexis let her head fall to the edge of the laptop. Time was ticking. She knew the law would allow Chief Spencer to hold Gerald for only eight hours to question him about Theresa and the drug ring since his trespassing charge wasn't likely to stick.

"They picked Gerald up sometime between eight thirty and nine at night, when the fireworks started. Unless the chief finds some other reason to hold him, we have until only five in the morning to find some evidence. Our time is running out."

# TWELVE

Nick tossed and turned on the couch. His exhaustion should've meant he could have slept anywhere, but his mind wouldn't turn off. Alexis had pinpointed his unease with his campaign. While he could encourage changes to be made in the town to stop drug use, he couldn't control people. He could provide more resources for recovery and officers in the schools, but it didn't mean that the town's drug problem would be cured. He sat up in a cold sweat. So was it a waste of time?

His brother had to have faced the same issue, but he had seemed to have an easier time compartmentalizing his work and life. Rarely did he ever talk about work, except if Nick had pestered him with questions whenever they were together. From Nick's perspective, his brother's job had seemed more important than his own.

He looked up at the ceiling as the truth hit him. Even before his brother's death, Nick had been looking for contentment and his identity in other places besides the true source. If he could just be more, control more…

*Forgive me, Lord.* His entire life as he knew it threatened to fall apart. It was about time he put his identity in the right place. Because if Alexis's friend couldn't help them figure out the puzzle of the time cards, Nick was ready to turn himself in. His confidence had to come from the Lord.

*Why couldn't I have met her at a different time?* Alexis stirred his heart in a way no other had before. He wanted to get to know her better without running for their lives. Not that it would be easy even if their names were cleared. Alexis didn't believe that he wouldn't have other political aspirations. She refused to let them have a chance because of her past. How would he ever convince her that he didn't care about that? He cared more about their future.

He shuffled into the kitchen and put on a pot of coffee. While it percolated, he looked around, hoping to get his mind off the situation. A box of files sat on the edge of the counter with Raven's toys and training items. Raven's name was on the front of the files. He pulled them out, curious if they would contain a clue about Raven's future owner.

Flipping a folder open, he recognized the first set of papers as a copy of her medical report. He made sure his clients left with a set of them after each visit. It lessened the chance of confusion about what he'd said during an appointment if they had his notes in print. Behind that was a log of Raven's training schedule and benchmarks. What must have been Joe's scrawled handwriting was all over the place.

6/15 Works for approval more than toys or treats. Extraordinary detection of narcotics.

8/3 Excels at detection. Other elements of police work don't interest her.

8/15 Training exercise proved she will protect me but refuses to attack others. She's a lover, not a fighter.

Nick chuckled but sobered at the next line written just before the hit-and-run.

9/1 Starting to wonder if Raven would be better suited as a therapy dog.

A brochure on therapy dog training had been paper-clipped to the back of the folder. Nick pulled it out to read it but noticed that Raven no longer lay at the base of the couch. Come to think of it, he didn't remember stepping over her when he got up to get coffee. When was the last time he heard her deep breathing? Maybe that was part of the reason he couldn't sleep well. Had she gone out the doggie door?

He started to walk to the back door when something buzzed. Finding Raven would have to wait a second. He followed the buzzing into the hallway. Through the open door of a bedroom, he spotted Alexis sleeping, fully clothed, on top of the comforter with her arm draped over Raven. Her peaceful face was even nuzzled up against the dog's fur.

His shoulders relaxed, and he put a hand over his mouth so he wouldn't laugh aloud. If she hadn't claimed to hate dogs so much, the image would've been heartwarming more than hilarious. Raven lifted her head and turned to look at him as if to say, *Would*

*you make that buzzing racket stop before it wakes
her up?*

He crossed the room and peeked at the offending smartphone on the nightstand. He hated to wake
her up, but this was the call they'd been waiting for.
"Alexis. It's Victoria."

She sat up in one smooth motion and swung her
legs off the bed. Raven jumped off the bed with a har-
rumph and rested at her feet. Alexis blinked. He didn't
take the time to let her wake up fully but handed her
the phone. She frowned, put her thumb on the answer
button and lifted it to her ear. "Hello?"

"Sorry. Did I wake you?" The voice on the other
end was loud enough Nick could hear it. "I thought
you said it was urgent. I woke up and saw the tons of
messages you left."

Nick glanced at the clock on the wall. Seven in
the morning came quickly when you didn't go to bed
until two.

Alexis closed her eyes. "Um, yeah. It is urgent."
She yawned. "Let me put you on speakerphone."

She pressed the button and rested the phone on the
bed. "Okay," Victoria said, "so I'm looking at these
time cards. Totally old school. Did you say this guy
was an investment banker?"

Alexis looked as if she'd fallen back asleep even
though she was sitting up straight.

"Uh, yes," Nick answered.

"Bookkeeping is one thing, but I don't understand
how he would be able to keep up with investments and
stock markets without being technologically savvy."

"Well, he does have computers," Alexis said. "He
just doesn't like them. I'll admit it might be something

the police should look into, but he doesn't come across as smart enough to pull anything dodgy."

"Hmm." Victoria didn't sound so certain. "My fraud senses are going off, but without doing a full audit on him, these time cards don't tell me much. Though I did wonder why only some of them have extra numbers."

Alexis stood up. "Extra numbers? What do you mean?"

Alexis ran to the laptop and pulled up the images.

Victoria rattled off instructions. "Check the one for June 20, when you filled in for receptionist at the medical practice. Then look at July 15. Then there's one in August—"

"I see them," Alexis said. She zoomed in on the images. Sure enough, there was an extra set of numbers on each of them listed underneath Project Number. She'd assumed that was a reference for bookkeeping purposes, but it had to be more than that. None of the other time cards utilized the project number section. And even if they had, not all of her time cards with the medical practice listed a project number. She did the same job, though, each time she worked there.

"A code?" Nick asked.

"Maybe," Alexis said. "Or maybe it's something for their personal records. A medical practice would have different paperwork needs."

"Something about it is niggling in the back of my mind," Victoria said over the speakerphone. "I can't figure it out, though."

"Can't figure what out?" a deep voice in the background said.

"I'm on the phone with Alexis. It's Jeff," Victoria said into the phone. "These numbers."

"If they didn't have those extra numbers after the slash, I'd almost think they were GPS coordinates," Jeff said.

"Did you hear that?" Victoria asked.

Nick leaned forward and put his finger on the laptop screen. "These don't look like GPS coordinates to me."

Alexis agreed. The first number had a double digit, a decimal point and a long line of numbers followed by a vertical slash. The second set was a negative double-digit number, a decimal point and a long line of numbers. The third set after the slash was a series of eight numbers.

"There are different ways of listing coordinates," Jeff explained. "Most people are used to seeing the little degree symbol and a set of cardinal directions—north and south along with east or west. We call that the DMS method, but another method is to give latitude and longitude. Latitude always goes first. I have no idea what the third set of numbers would be, though."

Alexis leaned forward. Because of Jeff's skydiving business, it made sense that he would know how to decipher coordinates. Nick leaned over her shoulder and pulled up a browser. He typed in the first two sets of numbers from the June time card.

The first link that popped up said, "Barings, Idaho, Latitude and Longitude."

Nick leaned back and exhaled. "I think we might be getting somewhere. I would've never guessed that was anything other than a project number."

Her heart pounded. That was too big a coincidence to ignore. Jeff had to be on to something.

"If you want to be sure," Jeff added, "there are converters online that will turn it into standard DMS. Then you can plug that into Google Maps."

"So try that and let us know, okay? I'm getting ready to head out of town. Investigation in Portland," Victoria said. "I'm sorry I couldn't be of any more help."

Alexis passed on her thankfulness as Nick rapidly found an online converter. Within seconds, he'd determined the location. An agricultural sales warehouse on the outskirts of town. She stared at it, slack-jawed. Agricultural sales had nothing to do with a medical practice. But maybe they were barking up the wrong tree. "We still don't know what the third set of numbers could be."

"Let's try the other two extra number sets before we attempt to figure that out. See if the GPS thing was a fluke."

He typed in and converted the first two sets of numbers for the July and August time cards. Each time, they pinpointed an exact business, unrelated to the medical practice. She leaned back, staring at the map.

Nick tapped her monitor. "Okay, if we're running with this theory, we have to figure out the third set of numbers."

She stared at the June time card. It hit her all at once. "A date and time?"

Nick pointed at the numbers: 06240300. "June 24. Three in the morning if you're using military time."

His eyes lit with hopefulness as their gazes connected. "Did we figure it out?" She scrolled to the next odd time card in July.

"July 28 at six o'clock in the evening." Nick tapped the table. "It'd still be light out. That would be bold."

"Maybe it would draw less attention. Look at the location. It's the heating-and-air parts warehouse. Anyone there on a Saturday at that time wouldn't look so out of place. However, technicians might still be in their trucks servicing clients, but I know for a fact they close up shop by three o'clock on Saturday no matter what. I got tasked with locking up once."

Her fingers shook as she pulled up the August time card. Nick entered the coordinates. "That would be—"

She gasped as the location showed up on the browser. "Barings Furniture? I loved working there. Mr. Griggs is the nicest man. He can't be part of a drug operation. There's no way."

"We don't know if he's involved, Alexis. We're not even sure what this is."

"It has to be connected to the drugs and the mayor." She examined the rest of the numbers. "September 3, two o'clock in the afternoon." Her gaze lifted to meet Nick's. "That's today. Whatever it is, it's going down today."

He tilted his head back. Grabbing her hands, he pulled her to standing as if he wanted to jump up and down. "You did it. You figured it out."

"If we had more time cards from the past years, it would help confirm our theory. Gerald came into his newfound wealth a long time ago. So this must have been going on since then." She started to pace around the room. "Theresa always gave me first chance to work at the practice ever since I moved back. It was one of the nicer jobs so I always took it. But if we're right, the code had to be on other time cards of previous temps who worked there."

"So we don't know exactly what it means yet."

"We know enough. These time cards would've gone from Theresa to Barry for bookkeeping. So someone at the practice had to be feeding Barry the time and place the deals were going down. It's almost foolproof because it passes through several hands without any digital trace. It's the real reason Barry insisted on going old school." She held up a finger. "One of the part-time nurses at the practice hates her job. Said she's tired of looking at rashes all day, but there aren't many medical jobs in our town. She might be the contact supplying the numbers through all the temps."

"Do you think the other temps are in danger, then?"

"I hope not. There was high turnover. There are only a few temps who have worked for Theresa the past few months, and they're much older ladies. I doubt any of them felt the need to keep digital records like I did."

"So how is the bookkeeper involved?"

"Gerald and Barry are brothers. Gerald must have been using Barry's so-called investment service to launder the drug money."

He nodded. "Makes sense to me. We'll give this to the police, and they should be able to catch them red-handed."

Her cheeks hurt from how wide she grinned.

He pulled her into his arms for a hug. She closed her eyes for the briefest of moments, wanting to savor the moment. Because no matter how much she wanted to pursue a relationship with him, she'd come to terms with the fact she never could.

He released her, but only just enough that he could see into her eyes. "I'm glad you got some sleep…with the help of Raven."

She tilted her head. "Raven?"

Laughter shone from his eyes. "You two were pretty cozy on the bed. I think you've made a new friend."

She frowned. He had to be crazy. "I did no such thing. I would never allow a dog to sleep on the bed." Although, come to think of it, she did dream about wrapping herself in a fuzzy blanket.

"If you say so." He smiled. "Alexis, after we both get some real rest, I'd like to take you out for dinner."

Her heart plummeted. "I can't."

He released her and stepped back, confusion and hurt written on his face. "Why?"

"The problem with lawyers is they talk too much."

His forehead creased. "Why do I feel like you're leading the witness?"

"I made it pretty obvious I liked you, but without a gun pointed—"

His jaw dropped. "Oh, you can stop there." He shook his head as if trying to erase the conversation. "I see where this is going. If you need a gun pointed at you to want—"

"No, you don't know where I was going." Her words rushed out. "After we prove Gerald is guilty, this town will need a mayor. And in a couple years, this state will need a senat—" She let her sentence drop because it hurt to think she couldn't be alongside him. "I can't stand in the way of you changing the world for the better. I won't do that to another good man."

"There's a verse. I might butcher it, but basically it says if I understood all mysteries, all knowledge, had all faith so that I could move mountains yet have not love, then I am nothing."

Her heart stopped for a moment, savoring the words. She knew the passage. "I think that verse is about loving all mankind," she said softly.

He nodded as if he knew, as well. He squinted as he looked up at the ceiling. "There's something in Ecclesiastes. If one man falls, the other will lift him up. But woe to him that has no one—"

She grinned, appreciating his quick thinking. A lot of people couldn't keep up with her, but Nick practically outpaced her. "You're really reaching now, aren't you?" She laughed. "I appreciate the sentiment."

"Okay. Well, this comes straight from the book of me, myself and I. I'm working at trusting God more so I'm not upset by decisions people make that I don't agree with. But please hear me when I say that if the town doesn't choose me as their leader because I want a beautiful, kind woman with a servant's heart, who I think loves this town more than I do, to be by my side, then that's their bad decision. And I could accept that."

Her eyes filled with tears. It was so tempting. He had no idea. But she couldn't do that to him. Not in the long run. He said he could accept it, but what about five years from now? "I can't," she whispered.

# THIRTEEN

They crunched on cereal and sipped coffee in silence on separate sides of the room. It sounded like a symphony composed of awkward. Even if everything between them had been peaches and roses, the reminder that Joe wouldn't be returning to finish the milk before it went bad hung over Nick's head.

"If they ever find his next of kin, we should make a donation," Alexis said, as if thinking the same thing. "Can I use your phone?"

"Why?"

"Given my last conversations with Jeremy and Chief Spencer, I'm not sure they'll answer my call."

He doubted that was true but handed over the phone.

She pointed it at the monitor, snapped photos of the time cards and emailed them to the same address the officer at Theresa's office had supplied. *Here goes*. She dialed and pressed the speakerphone function.

The moment the chief answered, the words flew off her tongue, enough to rival any fast-talking auctioneer. She told him how to read the numbers and relayed her guess that it was probably a wholesale drug shipment of some sort to be picked up by drug dealers throughout town.

"That's in a few hours," he said. "I don't have time to get cooperation from agencies in other towns. We don't have a resident DEA or SWAT team, and frankly, you don't have enough evidence in these time cards for me to justify using one even if I wanted to."

Alexis slumped onto the couch. "Please. You know I'm innocent, Chief. I had access to a vehicle. If I were guilty, wouldn't I have fled town? You know in your gut someone killed Theresa and that scout and Joe. They weren't your typical overdoses. Their deaths have to be connected."

He harrumphed. "The hospital footage showed that Theresa entered Joe's room the night of his death."

Alexis's face paled. "You're not suggesting she—"

"It's possible she saw something. The images are grainy, but she argued with a doctor in the hallway who kept his face turned away from security cameras. The Boise Police have yet to find the doctor matching his description."

"Does he by chance look like Gerald?" Nick asked.

"Gerald is bald," the chief responded. "This man is not."

"His brother, Barry, has a full head of hair," Alexis added. "It makes perfect sense. He runs the bookkeeping service. Has the mayor talked yet? He was with Theresa. He has to know something."

An uncomfortable silence settled over the line. "We had to let him go."

"Then you need to follow up on this tip. Something is going to happen today at that furniture store.

And what about all those shootouts? Chief, that has to be enough."

He growled something under his breath. "Barry had an alibi. I know how to do my job. Come to the station."

She hung up on him and turned to Nick. "If he's not going to be at the drop-off, we can't prove our innocence. A drug test might prove we weren't taking drugs but not that we weren't in possession with the intent to distribute."

Nick pointed at his phone. "So maybe we film it happening."

"Yes. Now you're talking."

He shook his head. "While I appreciate your enthusiasm, there's no way I'm letting you get within a hundred feet of that furniture shop."

She eyed him and gave him a smile that he was beginning to regard as dangerous. "You said you wanted to help stop drug trafficking in this town."

It was, in fact, exactly what he wanted to do, but he'd never intended to be so hands-on about it, and he still wasn't sure it was the wisest option. He racked his brain for other ideas and came up with squat. "What we need is a good vantage point, and a promise from you that if this doesn't work, you'll accompany me to the safety of the police station. No matter what."

She pulled up the map on her own phone. "Help me find the perfect spot."


"Could you stop checking your phone? You're making me nervous." He peered out the window. "Unless it's to tell me the police are on the way."

She clicked off the screen as Nick resumed his pacing in front of the windows. "Sorry. I'm just checking the time again. Maybe we got it wrong. They're late." She'd never thought that her odd jobs for the temp agency would've been good for more than a low hourly wage. But the office space for lease above an insurance office made for the perfect spot to see the back of the furniture store.

All it had taken was one call to Jessica, a real-estate agent who Alexis had helped set up showings for a couple of times. Jessica was more than happy to supply the code to the lockbox so she could take a peek at the office space. "It's about time you set up your lawyer digs in town," Jessica had said.

Alexis had tried to lightheartedly shut down the lawyer practice idea, but Jessica had merely laughed. "It'll be our little secret. Check it out and let me know what you think."

Raven paced in front of the folding chair. Alexis reached down and rubbed her soft ears.

"She's growing on you," Nick said.

Alexis shrugged. "She's not bad, I guess. For a dog." Tears threatened to overcome her out of nowhere. How could an animal show such undying devotion to someone it'd only recently met? It moved her. "I wonder who will get her."

Raven wagged her tail as if she understood. The hair near the dog's neck spiked as she stiffened. Alexis pulled her hand back, at first wondering if she'd touched Raven's stitches. But she'd been nowhere near the spot. She looked around but saw nothing. The rev of a motor sounded.

"Here we go," Nick whispered, as if the vehicle could hear them. He ducked and lifted his phone to the corner of the window and pressed Record. Alexis leaned forward, keeping her head low but still high enough that she could see through the window as the furniture truck rounded the corner and headed for the back of the store.

"Do you see the police?" She tried to keep the fear out of her voice, but if they couldn't see Gerald or any criminal activity from the window, then they would still be without evidence. Her heart plummeted as the steel door to the store's loading dock rolled up and the truck backed into it. "I didn't see the driver or whoever opened the door. Did you? I really thought the chief would come around, and the cops would be here."

Nick's head dropped, and he stopped recording. "We tried, Alexis. I think it's time to give up."

Raven released a growl that sent chills up Alexis's spine. It sounded more like a mama bear than a dog. She spun around.

"I agree with him." Barry stood at the top of the stairway, pointing a gun at them. With bushy eyebrows hanging low over his blue eyes, a constant five-o'clock shadow, and dark, thick, wavy hair, he would've more aptly been named Harry. "It is time for you to give up, Alexis."

Her insides twisted. "I genuinely didn't think it was you." She shook her head, but her indignation that this man would pose as a friend to Theresa rose past the fear. "Why would you kill Theresa?"

He reared back as if he'd been slapped. "I didn't do that. I would never do that."

"Yeah, and I'm sure you didn't kill Joe, either, or set us up."

His eyes widened. "I didn't kill anyone."

"Yeah, so the police told me." She huffed. "Your so-called alibi. Someone in your drug ring lied for you, huh?"

He waved the gun wildly. Raven made a sound between a bark and a whine. Alexis's breath caught. Maybe she'd gone too far, but if they were going to admit defeat and die anyway, she at least wanted to know the whole truth. Nick took a step forward and twisted his body as if to block her from any bullets. The gesture was enough to make her words run dry.

"Leave Jessica out of this," Barry spat.

It was a good thing she'd been too stunned to speak. So that was how Barry knew where they were. Jessica, the real estate agent, and Barry were an item. Another unlikely pairing, but she felt sure that, like Theresa, Jessica had no idea what kind of man she'd become involved with.

Barry's face turned red. "And she's not part of any drug ring, either. I'm just here to escort you. So shut your smart mouth and do what I say. I don't want to hurt you." He looked at Nick, eyes imploring. "I never wanted anyone to get hurt." His voice shook with emotion.

Alexis turned to Nick, whose face mirrored her own confusion. Barry had the appearance of someone helpless and in sorrow, just as Gerald had.

"What are you and your brother mixed up in?" Nick asked. "Maybe we can help."

"Mind your own business and get moving."

"The police will be here any minute. We told them all about this."

Barry raised an eyebrow. "So you were the reason for the unplanned traffic stop. Well, nice try. All they saw was furniture inside the truck." He gave a pointed look at the dog. "Without a sniffer, they wouldn't find the drugs stashed inside. They gave the men the green light and moved on, which is what you need to do right now."

Her heart sank. No one would be coming to the rescue.

Barry took a side step and waved them out of the office space. Instead of going down the stairs, he pointed them into the hallway to the fire escape. Raven automatically walked on Alexis's left side, on the opposite side of Barry, as they passed him. Any hope Alexis had that the dog had a hero's instinct faded away.

Once outside, she desperately looked for someone, anyone, who could call for help. Barry pulled his gun closer into his side, but no one was on the sidewalk, on the street or in the alley between the buildings. From this vantage point, she could see a small space between the loading dock and the furniture truck, but there was no sign of anyone. Her eyes filled with tears. Why would God give her a desire to advocate for the less fortunate, yet when she needed a defender, leave her helpless?

She tripped on one of the grated steps, but Nick grabbed her arm to keep her from falling farther. She swiped her vision clear. Maybe she wasn't being fair. Events hadn't gone the way she'd thought they should have, but she had never really been alone. Her parents had been there for her when she'd been disbarred, and maybe if she'd been humble enough and let others know, some of them would've been as supportive as Nick. He had been there when her car almost dove off a cliff and when a bullet had been aimed at her. Twice. And maybe God would've defended her if she'd laid down her fear and gone into the station when Nick had asked her to.

"I'm sorry," she whispered to him. "You were right. I should've given up sooner. I should've listened to you."

Nick gave her a rueful smile as they continued to descend the stairs. "Just remember that if we get out of this—" he winked and reached for her hand "—I think I've fallen in love with you."

Warmth filled her chest, but she couldn't afford even a moment to enjoy it.

Nick gave her fingers a squeeze before she pulled away. They reached the bottom of the stairs and crossed the alley. If they were going to die, at least she could face death with hope in her heart.

# FOURTEEN

Nick tensed as he opened a nondescript door from within the alley. While Barry claimed he didn't want to kill them, they had no guarantees about the motives of whoever waited on the other side of the door.

The tip of the gun pressed into Nick's back. "Go on," Barry urged.

The back wall was aqua with black letters in the middle spelling Barings Financial Advisors. The name seemed odd, as Barry was the only advisor at the firm. Texturized taupe wallpaper covered the rest of the walls. Two black leather couches were on opposite sides of the room. They walked toward the empty receptionist desk. Maybe if Nick was fast enough, he could dial 911 from the landline.

Barry gasped behind them. Nick spun around. Someone wearing blue surgical gloves had an arm around Barry's throat. The man inserted a needle into the side of his neck before Barry could even struggle.

Barry's eyes went wide before his mouth and body went slack. The man let go of his throat and grabbed the gun from his hand as Barry's form dropped to the floor.

He calmly capped the syringe.

"You," Alexis breathed.

Dr. Tindale smiled. "Here I am."

Nick warred between rage and confusion. "Why? You're a doctor!"

He smirked. "It's a new generation. Operating a profitable drug ring that skates underneath the nose of law officials takes the same professional skills as managing a successful practice."

Alexis shook her head. "You already make—"

"Beans." Spittle escaped his mouth, an unattractive feature for a man who clearly spent too much time grooming his wavy hair. "A dermatologist in a small town that was supposed to have thrived and has only shrunk. Many of the operators I know have—" he shrugged "—decent paying jobs, I suppose. But if I want the lifestyle I deserve, heroin is the future. And despite living in this Podunk town, it's slightly bigger than all the other small towns in the area. A virtual hub."

"Your stuff is deadly," Nick interjected.

"For those who want the bigger high, they have to accept the bigger risk. We use only microscopic amounts for my regular customers. Obviously, Barry wasn't a regular."

Raven took a step toward the man, and then jumped back, barking.

Tindale waved the gun, directing it at Raven. "That dog was supposed to be dead by now. As soon as Joe brought this rat with him to his appointment, I knew it had to go. It was sniffing and barking. Joe tried to lie and claim the dog was still in training, but I knew he suspected me. They both had to go."

"You were behind the hit and run. You were the doctor at the hospital." Alexis put a hand to her mouth as she yanked back the leash to pull Raven behind her. She stood in front of the dog, and Raven sat at attention. "Theresa spotted you there."

"How was I to know they'd come visiting?" The doc shrugged.

"She'd have known it was you who killed Joe," Alexis said.

Nick tried to step in front of Alexis, but the doctor pointed the gun at him. "Stay there. Gerald said he would keep her in line, but it became clear she was a liability. I'm six months away from retiring for good on a Caribbean island. I just need a few more deals. So if you don't want to end up like your friend..." He stepped to the side and gestured for Alexis to move away from the dog.

She shook her head. Dr. Tindale's eyes narrowed. "You should be able to understand, Alexis. You lose your license in one state, it makes it harder to practice in another."

Her eyes widened.

"Yeah, I looked you up the first time you came into my office." He pursed his lips. "If you'd taken the time to know me, you'd have found we have a lot in common."

Bile rose in Nick's throat. "She was trying to bring justice and healing to others. I imagine all you've done is help yourself." Nick fisted his hands.

The doctor held up the syringe. "The first time you see someone die in front of you is the hardest, but—" he waved it a little "—this stuff makes it pretty easy. I sensed Barry's gratitude was waning after I'd taken him from small-time bookkeeper to investment manager." He sighed. "But the good news is, neither of you has to die."

Nick and Alexis exchanged a glance. What did he mean?

"It's simple," Tindale continued. "Alexis writes a statement that the veterinarian was behind it all." He shrugged and cast a smile at Nick. "You'll have to go to prison, but you understand. It's the only way."

"Then what?" Alexis pressed. "You let me walk?"

"Oh, no. That wouldn't do me any good. No, you'll take over Barry's job. There will be some that won't trust you since you're disbarred, but most people won't bother changing a thing as long as their dividend checks come regularly. Which they will. We'll probably even have them increase a bit to stop questions. Then, if you'd like, you can choose to come with me or stay here in this pit stop."

Nick's breathing grew erratic. He couldn't be serious. What would stop Alexis from turning witness the moment he was out of sight? And forget about being disbarred, she didn't have a background in finance. His plan didn't make sense.

She pointed toward the sign taped to the receptionist desk. "I can't just step into Barry's role. What about the Securities Investor Protect—"

"Do you think people actually check to see if their brokers are members of SIPC or FINRA?" He shook his head. "Hasn't happened yet. People believe what they want to believe."

"Fine. I'll do whatever you want. But you leave the dog alone." She threw her shoulders back. "I'll make sure she doesn't go into detection work."

"Give him the dog and start writing."

She handed the leash handle to Nick and rounded the desk, her features determined. Tindale stayed right behind her, hovering over her even as she sat down in the chair. He dictated everything for her to write down.

Why would Tindale trust that she wouldn't testify against him? The only thing making sense was that he would have something in writing blaming the two of them. There was no way Tindale would let them live. It had to be a ruse.

Alexis sighed dejectedly. She closed her eyes briefly before she signed her name at the bottom.

"Thank you, dear." In one swift motion, Tindale flicked the cap back off the syringe and aimed it for her neck.

Raven leaped in the air before Nick could register what was happening. She tugged the leash so violently it fell from his fingertips.

Raven's jaw snapped onto Tindale's forearm. She whipped her head back and forth and Tindale howled, but the man still managed to hold onto the needle. He screamed as he turned the gun in his other hand toward the dog.

Alexis leaned to the side, horror on her lips. She grabbed the stapler on the desk and smashed it upward into Tindale's arm holding the gun. The gun shifted and went off. A bullet soared through the ceiling, and fiberglass pieces rained down on the floor.

Nick jumped onto the desk. "Hit him in the face."

Alexis didn't need to be told twice. She smacked the stapler hard directly into Tindale's face as Nick wrenched the gun out of the man's hands. Tindale tried to shake the dog off his forearm. "Get him off!"

Nick handed the gun to Alexis. "Point it at him. If he so much as moves, shoot him."

Nick grabbed the man's wrist and squeezed while he pulled the syringe safely out of Tindale's hand.

"Just get it off," Tindale screamed again.

Three men in red hats and shirts with the logo Barings Furniture embroidered on them rushed in with guns drawn. "Police," one shouted.

Alexis did a double take but didn't drop the gun. "Jeremy?"

The man closest to her nodded and signaled the other two men to go around the desk and surround Tindale. She held out the gun for Jeremy to take. "You guys were there all along?"

"Alexis, can you call Raven?" Nick asked, a smile on his face. "She's not listening to me."

Raven's hind legs were on the desk, but she still whipped her head side to side, her mouth firmly embedded in Tindale's arm. "Here, girl."

Raven's ears perked. She dropped fully onto the desk and vaulted to Alexis's side. Nick joined Alexis and put a hand on her back. "Are you okay?"

"The moment I started writing, I knew he was never going to let us go. He was setting it up so it looked like a murder-suicide so he could go on with business as usual. If it weren't for you, Raven and the police…" Her throat closed so she couldn't say any more. She'd never been so thankful.

Jeremy holstered his weapon once the other two officers had Tindale in hand. "We pulled the furniture truck over on a traffic stop. The two drivers had rap sheets longer than my arm. So we took over and helped the dealers in the store unload the furniture. They started pulling out packages of drugs. Must've been hundreds of thousands of dollars' worth." He smirked. "We arrested ten dealers without so much as a bullet fired, and that was my first undercover assignment."

"Good work. Check the doc for more syringes," Nick called out to the other officers as they escorted him out the door. "Carefully."

Jeremy nodded at Nick. "Thanks."

Chief Spencer walked in at that moment and headed straight for Alexis. He reached his hand out and shook his finger at her. "You have caused me more grief…" He pulled her into a surprising bear hug. "I'm thankful you're safe. If anything had happened to you, your dad would've had my hide."

Tears stung her eyes at the unexpected display of affection. She blinked them back. "Gerald and Barry were both working for Dr. Tindale. I think they got in over their heads, but they were still involved."

The chief nodded. "I imagine Gerald will want to make sure the doc pays for killing his brother. He'll come clean." He reached out to Nick for a hearty handshake. "And I have a feeling you'll make a good mayor."

"You think he still has a chance?" Alexis asked. "After the news?"

"You two have been proven innocent." The chief frowned. "You mean because you were disbarred? Pfft. Most of the town knew a year ago."

"What?" She gazed at Nick in disbelief. He flashed what looked like a happy *I told you so* grin.

Jeremy crossed his arms over his chest. "Old news. I think I heard a good ten months ago."

Her mouth fell open. "You all knew? No one said anything!"

"What was there to say?" The chief shrugged. "Did you make a mistake? I don't know. Some say yes. Maybe there was a better way or maybe there wasn't. None of us could say. No one can fault your motivation, though. We just wanted to give you your space."

The whole town talked about and debated her situation?

Jeremy nodded. "Yeah, we figured you'd snap out of it when you were ready. It was none of our business."

She waited to see if he saw the irony of his statement, but he said nothing. A new thought struck her. "Did—did Theresa know, you think?"

Jeremy nodded. "Absolutely."

She gripped Nick's hand for support, to anchor her and keep the tears at bay. Theresa had been the one who offered her a job that proved to be a lifeline in her darkest hours. In fact, there had been plenty of support all around if she'd only seen it. The past year had been a prison of shame entirely of her own making. While the road ahead wasn't necessarily going to be smooth or without consequences, she would shift her focus where it belonged. She would keep looking up for guidance and hope.

Nick dropped down to check Raven's teeth and stitches.

The chief addressed him. "We haven't found a next

of kin for Joe. While you were at his house, did you figure out who the dog's owner would be?"

"You knew where we were?" Alexis asked.

Chief raised an eyebrow. "My cousin lives next door to Joe. She saw a dog in his backyard at eight in the morning and let me know." He looked slightly bashful admitting it next to a wide-eyed Jeremy. "Since you'd already called me, I chose to give you a few more hours. Face it, Alexis, there are no secrets in this town."

Nick laughed and reached down to ruffle Raven's ears. "Unless you find a will, there's no plan set in place for Raven's ownership. But I have someone in mind who would be a good fit."

Alexis's stomach plummeted at the thought. The dog had just saved her life, and they were already talking about sending her off somewhere else? "You aren't going to adopt her? Continue her training?"

Nick's eyes softened as he regarded her. "I hadn't planned to. Joe actually thought she might be better suited to something else. Though if we ever find that silver car, I would like to take a crack at it with her."

The chief stuck his lower lip out in thought. "Are you talking about the one involved in a shootout last night? We found it around the corner in a dark spot in the alley."

"Do you have cause to search it?"

"Yes, but we didn't find anything."

Nick grinned. "Let us try."

Nick knew his brother would've been happy that he'd paid so close attention to all the DEA stories he had told. As soon as Raven sniffed the car, she barked again at the spot underneath the passenger seat.

"We already looked there," Jeremy said.

Nick sat in the driver's seat and began pressing buttons in random order. The chief stood at the window, an amused grin on his face until Nick pressed the AC button and pushed the cigarette lighter in at the same time. A trapdoor underneath the floorboard popped open. Inside were several prefilled syringes, a fake passport with Dr. Tindale's photograph, cash and a bag presumably filled with heroin.

Nick strode over to meet Alexis. She grinned. "You sure you don't want to continue training her for detection?" She took a knee and wrapped her arms around Raven. "You two made an impressive team." Her eyes looked so hopeful, he couldn't wait to broach the subject any longer.

Nick reached into his jeans pocket and pulled out the folded therapy brochure. She opened it and stared at it in confusion. "Apparently Joe thought she would be a good fit for this. There are tons of practical benefits in taking a therapy dog with you when you work with or visit the elderly."

Her mouth dropped open and she stood up. "Me? You had me in mind for Raven?"

In that moment he knew he had made the right decision, but he tried to act nonchalant. "I couldn't adopt her. This girl I've fallen for made it pretty clear that owning a dog would be a deal breaker."

Her eyes lit up. "Did she? Well maybe she might be willing to reconsider."

A motor revved and screeched to a stop in front

of them. Nick tried not to groan in frustration at the interruption.

"Mr. Kendrick!" A man leaned out the window. "*Barings Herald*. According to police, you played a part in helping take down the drug ring in town. How do you think this will affect your campaign?"

Alexis stepped in front of Nick. "Hello, Tommy. This incident only proves that Nick Kendrick challenges the status quo and will make this town better for it." She leaned forward. "That's Alexis Thompson, campaign manager."

Nick's mouth dropped. "Tommy, is it? Will you excuse us?"

He led Alexis away from peering eyes. "Campaign manager, huh?"

Her cheeks and neck turned a rosy blush. "If the job is still available." She held up a hand. "I'll do it only on a volunteer basis. I refuse to be paid. And I'll have to work around my other responsibilities like getting certified for dog therapy, applying to the Idaho Bar…"

His neck tingled with the spark of hope. He picked up her hand gently. "Are you sure? It'll probably involve a lot of lunches, late-night dinners, lots and lots of discussions."

She grinned. "You've already convinced me. There's something you should know, though."

"Oh?" His stomach churned with anxiety, knowing he'd already made it clear how he felt about her. If she insisted they'd never be more than friends, he'd respect her decision. He'd hate it, but he'd honor it.

She stared directly into his eyes. "Nick, I've fallen in love with you, too."

# EPILOGUE

*Three months later*

Alexis drove her new-to-her all-wheel-drive Honda CR-V up the hill. After months of driving back and forth to Nick's house to take horse riding lessons—her new favorite exercise—the curves no longer scared her. She could appreciate the beauty of the road, even in the winter. She pulled over to the viewing point.

In the distance, she could see Nick a few feet past the railing, on the bench. Bundled in his blue North Face coat, complete with a knit beige scarf, he looked picture perfect. She tightened the belt on her red wool trench coat and let Raven out of the backseat. Raven looked up expectantly, wagging her tail.

"Go on, then."

Raven bounded into the light dusting of snow toward Nick. The dog was so well trained, Alexis didn't even need to put a leash on her. Alexis followed her and sat next to Nick. "Hello, Mayor Kendrick."

"I got some good news that the K9 grant for the

town will be approved." He leaned over and kissed Alexis on the cheek.

Raven released a funny moan like she was annoyed at the display. Nick echoed the noise as if they were having a conversation about it. He handed Alexis a paper cup filled with hot chocolate, topped with whipped cream. "So, how'd Raven do on her first time out?"

After several classes with Raven, Alexis and the dog had been certified as a therapy team. While Alexis waited for the results of her appeal to the Idaho State Bar, she had no reason not to start serving the elderly in town. Today was their first visit at the nursing home. "Are you kidding? Raven was a natural. Everyone loved her."

"So Raven got plenty of affection. Then maybe she can spare some."

He leaned over and placed one hand on Alexis's neck and the other on her jaw. A shiver ran up her spine, and she was pretty sure it wasn't from the cold.

Raven jumped up on the bench and squeezed her way in between them. Nick sighed. "Raven, I lost something out here." He pulled out a glove from his pocket. The dog sniffed it heartily. "Go to work!"

Alexis frowned. "I didn't realize she knew how to go after a scent without being trained for it." Alexis leaned forward and examined the terrain. They could see the entire valley from this vantage point. "Do you think she'll be safe?"

"I won't let her go far. I have a feeling she knows this path well."

True to his word, Raven stuck her nose into the

snow near some sagebrush. She bounded back toward them with a black glove in her mouth.

"How did your glove get clear over there?"

It was almost as if Raven had played this game before with Nick. Before Alexis could ask a follow-up question, Raven dumped the wet glove in her lap. Except it felt too heavy against her leg to be just a glove, and it had an odd shape. Her breath caught. She looked to Nick for some kind of explanation.

He avoided eye contact and pointed at it. "What'd she find?"

Alexis stretched the opening of the glove and pulled out a velvet box. She stared at it instead of opening it. What if she was making an assumption that wouldn't prove true? Maybe it was just a necklace. "Nick…"

He dropped to a knee and opened the box for her. Inside, the square-cut diamond on the white-gold ring glistened. He reached to hold her hand. "Alexis Thompson, when I ran into you that first day, I knew I'd met my match."

She enjoyed the double meaning and knew it was true for her, as well. The last months had been filled with evenly matched debates over nonimportant issues. On the things that were really important, they heartily agreed. She equally loved their similarities and differences.

"My life changed forever, for the better," Nick said. "Will you make me the happiest man in the world and be my wife?"

She wanted to laugh and cry at the same time. "Yes," she whispered. Her gaze dropped to her hand in his. "I'm pretty sure a contract of this sort is supposed to be sealed with a kiss."

He stood and pulled her up with him. He gently brushed back her hair with his free hand and pulled her close to him. "I never argue with my lawyer."

His lips were half an inch away when she pressed her hand into his chest. "I hope that's not true."

"I see." He looked over her head as if searching for something to argue about. "Musicals are just long, drawn-out monologues."

"We'll have to go to one together to prove that's not true," she retorted.

He raised his eyebrows. "Um…it is never okay to be late."

Even though she agreed with him, she volleyed back for fun, "Then why is the term *fashionably late* a thing?"

He smiled and whispered, "White chocolate is better than dark chocolate."

She gasped and playfully hit his shoulder. "Too far!"

His laugh was delicious as he pulled her closer. "I love you, Alexis. I can't wait to be your husband."

She snuggled deeper into his embrace. "I love you, too."

Raven wormed her way between their legs. Nick groaned as he pulled out a dog treat from his pocket. "I'm ready for you." Raven took the treat and flopped down happily at their feet.

"Smart man. She deserves a lifetime supply of treats."

"Is that so?"

"Oh, yes. She not only won over a self-proclaimed

dog-hater but also went above and beyond and tracked
down the man of my dreams."

Nick looked into her eyes and beamed.

And finally, his lips touched hers.

\* \* \* \* \*

*If you enjoyed TRACKING SECRETS, look for
these other books by Heather Woodhaven:*

*CALCULATED RISK
SURVIVING THE STORM
CODE OF SILENCE
COUNTDOWN
TEXAS TAKEDOWN*

Dear Reader,

Over ten years ago, we moved across the country. Hoping to ease the sorrow of moving, my husband promised our three children that once we got settled we would get a dog. It took much longer than anticipated to find a home that suited our needs. So instead of summer, the children reminded their dad of his promise in January. I didn't consider myself an animal lover at the time. I mostly feared destroyed furniture and long periods of waiting in the frigid temperatures while housetraining a new dog.

Still, we took a trip to the animal shelter. To my surprise, there were many puppies available in the dead of winter. One by one we took each puppy into the pen. The moment we made it outside, the pups would run free. Until, that is, we escorted the last one outside. The final puppy had no interest in running around the square space. Instead, she nuzzled against each of us. We often tell people that we didn't choose a dog. She chose us. And she's been the perfect dog for our family. As you've probably figured out, she was the inspiration for Raven. I hope you enjoyed how she helped Nick and Alexis leave the past behind to enjoy a future together.

As always, I love to hear from readers. You can contact me and keep updated on new books through my newsletter at my website, WritingHeather.com.

Blessings,
*Heather Woodhaven*

# Get 2 Free Books,
## Plus 2 Free Gifts—
just for trying the
## Reader Service!

*A witness on the run must trust an FBI agent and his
K-9 partner to keep her safe.*

*Read on for an excerpt from Shirlee McCoy's
BODYGUARD,
the next book in the exciting new series
CLASSIFIED K-9 UNIT.*

If the Everglades didn't kill her, her uncle would.

Either way, Esme Dupree was going to die.

The thought of that—of all the things she'd leave
behind, all the dreams she'd never see come true—had
kept her moving through the Florida wetlands for three
days, but she was tiring. Even the most determined person
in the world couldn't keep running forever. And she'd been
running for what seemed nearly that long. First, she'd fled
witness protection, crisscrossing states to try to stay a step
ahead of her uncle's henchman. She'd finally found her
way to Florida, to the thick vegetation and quiet waterways
that her parents had loved.

Esme wasn't as keen. Her family had spent every
summer of her childhood in Florida exploring the wetlands.
She preferred open fields and prairie grass, but her parents
had loved the shallow green water of the Everglades. She'd
never had the heart to tell them that she didn't.

Funny that she'd come back here when her life was
falling apart. When everything she'd worked for had been

shot to pieces by her brother's and uncle's crimes, Esme had come back to a place filled with fond memories.

It was also filled with lots of things that could kill a person.

She wiped sweat from her brow and sipped water from her canteen. Things hadn't been so bad when she'd been renting a little trailer at the edge of the national park. She'd had shelter from the bugs and the critters. But Uncle Angus had tracked her down and nearly killed her. He would have killed her if she hadn't smashed his head with a snow globe and called the police. They'd come quickly.

Of course they had.

They were as eager to get their hands on her as Uncle Angus had been.

"You should have stayed with the police," she muttered. Maybe she would have if Angus's hired guns hadn't firebombed the place. She'd run again because she thought she'd be safer on her own.

Now she wasn't so sure.

*Don't miss*
*BODYGUARD by Shirlee McCoy,*
*available wherever*
*Love Inspired® Suspense books and ebooks are sold.*

www.LoveInspired.com

# lover in you!

Earn points from all your Harlequin book purchases from wherever you shop.

Turn your points into *FREE BOOKS* of your choice
OR
*EXCLUSIVE GIFTS* from your favorite authors or series.

Join for FREE today at
**www.HarlequinMyRewards.com.**

Harlequin My Rewards is a free program (no fees) without any commitments or obligations.

MYR17

## Love Inspired®

**Inspirational Romance to
Warm Your Heart and Soul**

Join our social communities to connect
with other readers who share your love!

Sign up for the Love Inspired newsletter
at www.LoveInspired.com to be the
first to find out about upcoming titles,
special promotions and exclusive content.

**CONNECT WITH US AT:**

Harlequin.com/Community

 Facebook.com/LoveInspiredBooks

 Twitter.com/LoveInspiredBks

LISOCIAL2017